CONFABULARIO
and other inventions

THE TEXAS PAN-AMERICAN SERIES

Confabulario

and Other inventions

by Juan José Arreola

translated by George D. Schade

ILLUSTRATED BY KELLY FEARING

UNIVERSITY OF TEXAS PRESS · AUSTIN

The Texas Pan-American Series is published with the assistance of a revolving publication fund established by the Pan-American Sulphur Company and other friends of Latin America in Texas. Publication of this book was also assisted by a grant from the Rockefeller Foundation through the Latin American translation program of the Association of American University Presses.

International Standard Book Number 0-292-73196-5 (cloth)
0-292-71030-5 (paper)
Library of Congress Catalog Card No. 64-13315

INTRODUCTION

In the last twenty years or so Mexican literature has been greatly enriched by the works of a group of extremely talented writers both in poetry and in prose. Octavio Paz (1914), Agustín Yáñez (1904), Juan Rulfo (1918), and Rosario Castellanos (1925) have already been translated into English and other languages and their work has been greeted with critical acclaim in Europe and the United States as well as in Mexico and other countries of the Spanish-speaking world. One of the most original and interesting writers among this generation is undoubtedly Juan José Arreola (1918), whose collected short stories, satiric sketches, bestiary, and sundry inventions are gathered together here under the general title *Confabulario*, which means a collection of fables.

Arreola, who has lived for many years in Mexico City, was born in Ciudad Guzmán in the state of Jalisco, Mexico in 1918. His stories first appeared in little magazines in Guadalajara in the early 1940's—one of them called *Pan* he edited with his friend Rulfo—and his first book, *Varia Invención*, came out in 1949. *Confabulario* followed in 1952, and in 1955 was published in a second edition together with *Varia Invención* in one volume. His bestiary appeared in 1958 under the title *Punta de Plata*. In 1962 these books, together with the addition of a large number of new pieces, were all brought out under the title *Confabulario Total, 1941-1961*.

This book is difficult to classify. Some of the pieces—like "The Switchman," "The Crow Catcher," "Private Life"—are clearly short stories in a modern mode, ranging widely in technique and style; a great many others, as the title would indicate, are fables; still others are sharp, satiric, one-page vignettes, and can hardly be called short stories. The tone and language vary considerably according to the subject. For example, in "Baby H.P." and "Announcement" Arreola parodies the commercial world of advertising, using jargonistic terms and a breathless tone with excellent effect. But the same marvelous invention and wit, the same trenchant satire, and impish, impudent humor run throughout the collection.

In an age when many writers take themselves so seriously as to be solemn, it is refreshing to come across an author like Arreola, who laughs gleefully and wickedly at man—and by implication, at himself—puncturing all the foolishness he indulges in and cutting through the glaze of manners society sets so much store by.

Arreola is an accomplished satirist. He is very good at finding chinks in the armor, attacking his subjects in their most vulnerable spots and sometimes in places where they probably did not realize they were vulnerable. Bourgeois society and all its false values, rampaging twentieth-century materialism, the bomb, the cocktail party are just a few of his targets. With mordant descriptions, pungent attacks, or sly irony, he shows how silly mankind is, how outrageous man's behavior and antics are, how one is at the mercy of a world and society that more often seems to care for what is trivial and ephemeral than for what is essential. Arreola jabs at complacency and ruthlessly exposes pompous and hypocritical attitudes.

He takes a depressing view of most human relationships, and in a large number of his stories and satires he chips away at love and its illusions. Like the celebrated seventeenth-century Spanish satirist Quevedo, Arreola is particularly hard on women and marriage. According to him, women are given to treachery and adultery, and the impossibility of finding happiness in marriage is a recurring theme and echo in his work. Whatever the subject of his satire, Arreola most often achieves his effects by a deliberate jumbling of phantasy and reality, a mingling of the logical and the absurd, a blend of imaginative frivolity and Orwellian grimness.

Arreola's range includes not only the present, but much of the past. He has a special penchant for medieval times, attested in such pieces as "The Song of Peronelle," "Sinesius of Rhodes," or "Epitaph," a short, sympathetic biographical sketch of the poet Francois Villon. Erudite allusions from other literatures and history crop up often in his prose, as well as learned references to writers and their works in other fields—anthropology, psychology, science. And he seems astonishingly knowledgeable about a variety of esoteric subjects, for example, Roman and other ancient war machines, which he describes in an hilarious story called "On Ballistics."

One of the most ingratiating and delightful parts of Arreola's collected works is his "Bestiary," consisting of twenty-six brief sketches. Here Arreola harkens back to that form which was so fashionable in medieval times with moralists and allegorizers, where certain virtues or characteristics were popularly atttributed to certain beasts, real or imaginary. All of Arreola's beasts are real, their humanlike foibles and defects uncomfortably real too. Though Arreola's general outlook and some of the details in his bestiary will probably horrify the overly sentimental, still there are lyrical and poetic touches to offset to some degree the refined savagery of his satire.

Endowed with a resilient mind that skims swiftly from point to point, Arreola is also a gifted stylist. His imagery and language, except in some of the earliest stories, are tart and fresh, his choice of words sometimes startling the reader, at other times stinging him, frequently delighting him. His writing is crisp with sentences that tend to be short and closely packed, yet there is no jerky or jolting effect; it is all perfectly under control, balanced and rhythmic. Anyone whose ear has become somewhat dulled by the monotone of much present-day literature will probably be charmed by the banquet in store for him in word and image in Arreola's prose.

Arreola has his quota of enthusiastic admirers; he has also his blinkered critics who upbraid him for turning his back on so-called Mexican themes. Of course, it is his enormous sophistication and universality that should attract readers of English, though he has done a few pieces very Mexican in theme and setting like "Ballad" and the impressive and touching story "The Crow Catcher," which should have an exotic appeal for the foreign reader.

Obvious attractions abound in these satires, but there are also subtle delights often lurking below the surface. One will find, for example, several levels of meaning in a story like "The Switchman," where the inadequacies of the Mexican railroad system are satirized on the obvious level; on a more symbolic level various interpretations of this story are possible.

If we wish to seek them, parallels to Arreola elsewhere are not difficult to find. "Small Town Affair" with its psycho-zoological tendency—a man assuming the attributes and horns of a bull—is somewhat reminiscent of Kafka's wretched character in "Metamorphosis" who awakens one morning to discover himself transformed into a gigantic insect. As the Mexican writer and critic Emmanuel Carballo has pointed out, several of Arreola's distinctive apocryphal biographies, including "Nabonides," "Balthasar Gérard," and "Sinesius of Rhodes," are inspired by Marcel Schwob's *Vies Imaginaires*. A contemporary author with whom Arreola is frequently compared is the Argentine Jorge Luis Borges, with his playful, extraordinarily penetrating intellect, brilliant imagination, and phantasmagoric stories (he has written a bestiary too). Going further back in time, we can cite other similarities: the icy wit and coarse, bawdy, macabre humor of Quevedo, or the cleverness and cynicism of Voltaire. But though we detect reminiscences of one writer and echoes of another in Arreola's work, there is no doubt that he has a voice of his own, an inimitable style of utterance,

With such a large number of stories, fables, and sketches—almost one hundred—some unevenness is bound to occur, but in my opinion, the shadows recede before the lights. There are brilliant pieces in *Confabulario* and the other books which really dazzle.

In this translation I have followed the text and arrangement of the 1962 *Confabulario Total* edition with several exceptions. I decided to exclude from this volume a one-act play, *La Hora de Todos*, first published in 1954, which seems to me ineffectual, greatly inferior to Arreola's prose fiction, and out of place in this collection. I made only one other cut, very reluctantly in this case, a short sketch in prose modeled on the French ballade with its three stanzas, each ending in a refrain, and an envoi. This ballade defied all efforts at coherent and smooth translation, the key phrase of the refrain being used in a series of plays on words through the text. A long and ponderous explanatory footnote would have been necessary, and this I rejected as unthinkable in Arreola. I have also taken the liberty of reversing the order of the first two parts in *Confabulario Total*, putting "The Bestiary" before "Prosody," for "The Bestiary" is a much more impressive opener. I do not think Arreola will find fault with this, as he himself shuffles many pieces about from *Varia Invención* to *Confabulario* and vice versa in the different editions of these books.

G.D.S.

TRANSLATOR'S ACKNOWLEDGMENTS

I wish to thank all those friends and colleagues who generously assisted me in the preparation of this book, especially Professor George Wing and Mrs. Elizabeth McGrosso, who read the manuscript and offered many valuable suggestions.

CONTENTS

PROSODY

CONFABULARIO

BESTIARY

Prologue

Love thy worthless, undeserving neighbor. Love thy neighbor who stinks, who is spotted with filth, who wears his poverty on his back.

Greet most heartily the grotesque fellow in sloppy pants who in the name of humanity gives you his trembling, jellylike credential, the dead-fish hand, all the while giving you the once-over with his big dog eyes.

Love thy neighbor, that pig, that rooster, who trots merrily along to his crude paradise—animal possession.

And love thy fellow woman too, who at thy side is suddenly transformed into somebody else, someone who in her cowlike pajamas interminably chews on the doughy cud of domestic routine.

The Rhinoceros

The rhinoceros comes to a halt. He raises his head. He backs up a bit. Then he wheels in a circle and fires his artillery piece. Furious and blind, a battering ram, he charges like an armored bull with a lone horn, with the single-minded vigor of a materialistic philosopher. He never hits the target, but he remains perpetually pleased with his strength. Then he opens his escape valves and snorts full steam. During the mating season the bull rhinoceroses repair to clearings in the forest. There, laden with excessive armor, they abandon themselves to the graceless, lumbering joust in which only the medieval clangor of the collision counts.

Now in captivity, the rhinoceros is a melancholy, rusty beast. His multiplated body was armed during prehistoric landslides with laminations of coarse hide and stamped under the pressure of geological strata. But at a special moment during the morning the rhinoceros startles us: from his dry, gaunt flanks, like water from the rocky cleft, springs the great organ of torrential and potent life. It repeats the horn motif of the beast's head, with variations of the orchid, the javelin, and the shield.

Let us pay homage, then, to the tough, abstruse creature, for he has given rise to a beautiful legend. Incredible though it may seem, this primordial athlete is the spiritual father of the poetic creature that is unfurled in tapestries of the Lady—the chivalrous, gallant unicorn.

Conquered by the prudent maiden, the carnal rhinoceros, transfigured, becomes deerlike, gazellelike, and kneels. And the obtuse horn of masculine aggression changes in the presence of the virgin to a svelte ivory lament.

The Toad

He hops from time to time just to prove his radical immobility. The hop is rather like a heartbeat; in fact, if you consider the matter carefully, a toad is all heart.

Pressed in a block of cold mud, the toad submerges himself in the winter like a pitiful chrysalis. He awakens in the spring, conscious that no metamorphosis has taken place. In his profound state of desiccation he is more of a toad than ever. Silently he awaits the first rains.

One fine day he emerges from the soft earth, heavy with humidity, swollen with rancorous juices, looking like a heart that has been flung to the ground. In the attitude of this living sphinx there is a secret offer to trade, and the toad's ugliness presents itself to our eyes with the oppressive quality of a mirror.

The Bison

Accumulated time. A mound of impalpable millennial dust, a sand-filled hourglass, a living glacier deposit: this is the present-day bison.

Before taking flight and leaving the field to us, the animals attacked for the last time, deploying the herd of bison like a horizontal battering ram. Since they maneuvered in compact masses, the bison seemed to be modifications of the earth's crust, each one looking like a small mountain, or in the guise of great swollen rain clouds, a storm scurrying across the surface of the land.

Without letting himself be swept along by that wave of horns, hooves, and snouts, man lay in ambush, shooting arrow after arrow, and one by one the bison fell. One day, seeing how few they were, they took refuge in the last Cenozoic sheepfold.

The peace pact founding our empire was signed with them. The tough, conquered bulls surrendered to us their bovine realm with all its reserves of meat and milk. And we put them to the yoke besides.

All of us are still enjoying the spoils of that victory: the last ounce of bodily strength we hold in reserve is precisely what we have assimilated from the bison. That explains why, in respectful homage, the primitive man in all of us produced as his best Altamira drawing the image of the bison.

Birds of Prey

A demolished medieval armory or a desecrated monastic cell? What is happening to the masters of free will?

Haughty heights and magnificent distances have suddenly taken on for them the dimensions of a modest chicken coop, a wire cage whose tin roof cuts them off from the pure contemplation of the heavens.

All of them, falcons, eagles, or vultures, like friars silently mouthing the Divine Office, repeat the boring Hours, while each day's miserable routine sets the stage for them with droppings and bland entrails: a sad morsel for their slashing beaks.

Gone forever are the great wheeling sorties, the soaring chase; gone forever the freedom to range between crag and cloud. Wing and tail feathers grow long in vain; talons grow sharper and ever longer in this prison, only to turn in upon themselves, like the rancorous thoughts of a once great nobleman.

But in the cage, all of them without fail, falcons, eagles, or vultures, endlessly wrangle over the prestige which springs from a common carnivorous ancestry. There are one-eyed eagles and hawks without a single feather.

The pure white King Vulture reigns supreme among all the coats of arms, his wings widespread over the carrion like ermine shields on an azure field, his head of chiseled gold set with precious stones.

Faithful to the spirit of a doctrinaire aristocracy, these rapacious birds observe to the limits of degradation the protocol of the barnyard. In this "Burke's Peerage" of nocturnal perches, each one occupies his place according to a rigid hierarchy and each of the great ones above stains in turn the escutcheon of those below.

The Ostrich

With a shrill cry, the ostrich's neck, like the pipe of a profane organ, proclaims to the four winds the radical nakedness of its flamboyant flesh. Since it could not be more lacking in spirit, the ostrich's whole body plays a series of impudent variations on the theme of modesty and shamelessness.

It is more like a gigantic diapered baby chick than a chicken. Doubtless the prime example of the shortest skirt and the most plunging neckline. Though always half-dressed, the ostrich makes an unnecessarily lavish display of its rags, and has gone out of fashion only in appearance. If its plumes are "no longer worn," elegant ladies willingly adorn their poverty with ostrich virtues and fripperies: the ostrich that puts on its finery but always leaves its ugly intimate parts uncovered. When something happens, if ostriches don't bury their heads, at least they shut their eyes to whatever is in the offing. With unequalled impudence they flaunt their jejune criteria and gobble up everything in sight, consigning it to the hazards of a good digestive conscience.

Clumsy, sensual, and arrogant, the ostrich represents the crowning absence of gracefulness, ever moving shamelessly in a seductive danse macabre. We should not, therefore, be surprised that the expert judges of the Holy Inquisition thought up the sport of tarring and feathering indecent women before thrusting them out naked in the public square.

Insectiad

We belong to a sad insect species, dominated by the supreme power of vigorous, bloodthirsty, terribly scarce females. For each of them there are twenty weak, sickly males.

We live in constant flight. The females pursue us, while for security reasons we abandon all nourishment to their insatiable jaws.

But the mating season changes the order of things. The females exude an irresistible aroma, and we, enervated, follow them to certain death. Behind each perfumed female trails a string of pleading males.

The spectacle gets under way when the female perceives that there are enough candidates. One by one we leap on her. With a quick movement she parries the attack and tears the gallant to bits. While she is busy devouring him, another aspirant flings himself on her.

And so on to the end. The union is consummated with the last survivor when the female, exhausted and relatively sated, scarcely has strength left to decapitate the male astride her, obsessed in his pleasure.

She remains asleep a long time, triumphant on her battlefield of mortal spoils. Then she hangs from a nearby tree a thick cartridge of eggs. From it the mass of victims will again be born with their unfailing complement of executioners.

The Water Buffalo

The carabao, or water buffalo, like Confucius and Lao Tse, interminably chews on the frugal cud of some eternal truths, obliging us to acknowledge once and for all the ruminant's oriental origins. True, water buffaloes are nothing but cows and bulls, and have little to justify their being shut up at the zoo. Visitors usually march right past their almost domestic animal look, but the keen observer stops when he sees that they look as if they were sketched by Utamaro.

And he meditates: long before the hordes led by the Tartar Khan, the Western plains were invaded by immense bovine herds. The extremes of that contingent were absorbed into the new landscape, little by little losing the characteristics that a study of the water buffalo now brings back to us: an angular development of the hindquarters and a deep-set tail, end of a protruding backbone reminiscent of the pagoda's plunging lines; long, straight hair; a general stylization of the shape somewhat approaching the reindeer's and the okapi's. Above all, the horns, frankly the buffalo's: wide and smooth at the base, joined over the head, then descending to the sides in a double, ample curve that seems to write the rounded word *carabao* in the air.

Felines

None of the following let themselves be impressed by appearances: the man who rescued Doña Juana's glove from the lion cage; Don Quixote, with real greatness of soul, who kept two beasts within bounds; Androcles, serene and without bombast (the lion no longer remembered the thorn); the martyrs who literally had to throw themselves into the hungry jaws; and the Viscount of the Asilos who ruined a Circensian spectacle by putting a sandwich into the King of the Forest's mouth. They have made the lion tamer's job, without whip or folding chair, lose standing in our day.

In reality the lion can scarcely bear the terrible majesty of his aspect: his body is not in harmony with his façade, and like his soul, is rather canine and seedy. He persists as a carnivore thanks to certain subjects who function as executioners for him. The lion presents himself in untimely fashion at savage banquets and, because of his regal primacy, puts the diners to flight. Then, alone and remorseful, he devours the remains of the prey he never personally captures. If they could choose, all the lions padding about the forest would be caged, tearing horse ribs and thighbones to pieces behind unnecessary bars. In short, they are never so happy as when made of marble and bronze or at least stamped on alarming circus posters.

Lacking a royal mane, many felines have to search for sustenance all on their own. This explains the undeniable superiority of tigers, panthers, and leopards, who sometimes manage to create a legend by attacking large livestock after scaring away their cowardly guardians.

If we did not domesticate all the felines we failed to do so simply for reasons of size, utility, and cost of maintenance. We have made do with the cat, who doesn't eat much and occasionally recalls his origin by giving us a little scratch. Only a few oriental princes can afford the luxury of owning larger felines that purr like a locomotive, are very useful as hunting dogs, and devour half the palace budget just by themselves. If they get distracted and scratch, they are capable of stripping any skeleton of all superfluous flesh.

The Bear

Between the open hostility of the wolf, for example, and the abject submission of the monkey, who is capable of sitting down with the family to breakfast at our table, stands the cordial moderation of the bear, who dances and rides a bicycle, but who can go too far and crush us in his embrace. It is always possible to strike up a friendship with him—at a distance—if we don't have a honeycomb in our hand.

Like his weaving head, the bear's soul weaves between slavery and rebellion. His pelt indicates his temperament: if white, bloodthirsty; if black, good-natured. Fortunately, the bear displays his different states of mind with all the nuances of grays and browns.

Whoever has met a bear in the forest knows that as soon as he sees us he stands up with a gesture of recognition and greeting. (The rest of the interview depends exclusively on us.) If women are involved, there is nothing to fear, since the bear has for them an age-old respect which clearly betrays his kinship with primitive man. However adult and athletic bears may be, they still have something babyish about them: no woman would refuse to give birth to a little bear cub. In any case, maidens always keep a furry teddy bear in their bedrooms as a good omen of maternity.

Let us confess: we have a common cave past with them. The cave bear yields the most abundant of fossils, and its distribution accompanies all prehistoric human migrations. In our day the bear den continues to be the most comfortable of wild lairs.

Latins and Teutons agreed in honoring the bear with a cult, baptizing with derivations of its name (*Ursus* and *Bera*) an extensive series of saints, heroes, and cities.

The Owl

Before devouring his victims the owl digests them mentally. He never takes a whole mouse under consideration without previously forming some idea of each one of its parts. The actuality of the throbbing victuals in his talons takes on a past concept in his mind and is a prelude to the analytical operation of a slow intestinal process. Here is a case of profound reflective assimilation.

With his sharply penetrating claws the owl directly apprehends his object and develops his peculiar theory of knowledge. The *thing in itself* (rodent, reptile, or flying creature) surrenders to him in some unfathomable way. Perhaps through the invisible claw-swipe of an instantaneous intuition, perhaps thanks to a logical period of waiting, since we always imagine the owl as stationary, introverted, and not much given to the predatory passions of chase and capture.

Who can say for sure that shadowy labyrinths, dark syllogisms that lead to nothingness after the brief clause of the beak, are not awaiting suitable creatures? To understand the owl is equivalent to accepting this premise.

Harmonious pillar of carved feathers perched on a Greek metaphor; sinister shadowy clock striking in the spirit an hour of medieval witchcraft: this is the two-faced image of the bird that flies at dusk and is the best vignette of books of Western philosophy.

The Elephant

The elephant comes from way back in time and is the last earthly model of heavy machinery, wrapped in its canvas sheath. It seems colossal because it is constructed with pure living cells and endowed with intelligence and memory. Inside the material accumulation of its body, its five senses function like precision instruments. Nothing escapes them. Though because of pure hereditary old age the elephant is now bald at birth, frozen Siberia has given us some woolly examples. How many years ago did the elephant lose its hair? Instead of trying to figure it out, let's all go to the circus and pretend we are grandchildren of the elephant, that childish grandfather who now sways to the rhythm of a polka . . .

No. Let's talk instead about ivory, that noble substance, hard and uniform, which pachyderms secretly push with all their body's might, like a material expression of thought. The ivory, which protrudes from the head and develops in the vacuum two curved, bright stalactites on which the Chinese with patient fantasy have carved all the elephant's formal dreams.

Moles

After long experience agriculturists have concluded that the only effective weapon against the mole is the hole. One must trap the enemy in his own system.

In the battle against the mole, holes are used now that reach to the earth's volcanic center. The moles fall in them by the dozens and, needless to say, die carbonized.

Such holes have an innocent appearance. Moles, who are short-sighted, are easily confused by them. Rather, one should say they prefer them, guided by a profound attraction. They are seen sol-

emnly filing toward a frightful death, giving a vertical dénouement to their intricate customs.

Recently it has been demonstrated that one definitive hole suffices for every six hectares of infested land.

The Camel Family

The llama's hair is impalpably soft, but its tenuous locks are chiseled by the harsh wind of the mountains where it struts about arrogantly, lifting high its svelte neck, so its eyes will be filled with distance and its fine nose absorb at an even higher level the supreme distillation of rarefied air.

At hot sea level the camel seems a small asbestos gondola with its four feet slowly rowing through the waves of sand while the desert wind pummels the massive sails of its humps.

For the thirsty, the camel guards in its rocky insides the last trickle of humidity; for the solitary, the plushy, curving, feminine llama assumes the movements and grace of an illusory woman.

The Boa

The boa's proposition is so irrational that it immediately seduces the rabbit before the latter can give its consent. A little massage and superficial salivary lubrication are scarcely necessary.

The rabbit, easily fascinated, surrenders to asphyxiation without a struggle. Its head and front feet disappear. But when half-swallowed, it feels the anguish of death. An aid to the boa are the rabbit's last live moments, advancing and disappearing while being propelled into the riblike tunnel with gradually more and more tenuous death rattles.

Then the boa realizes what grave responsibilities it has assumed and begins its digestive struggle, the real battle against the rabbit, which is attacked from the periphery to the center with abundant secretions of gastric juice, embalming it in successive layers. Fur, skin, tissues, and viscera are carefully treated and dissolved by the stomach's machinery. Finally the skeleton is submitted to a cracking and crushing process by means of contractions and lateral poundings.

After several weeks the victorious boa, having survived a long series of intoxications, abandons the last remnants of the rabbit in the form of laboriously polished, tiny chips of bone.

The Hippopotamus

Pensioned off by nature and bereft of a swamp his size, the hippopotamus sinks into boredom.

Biological potentate, he no longer keeps company with the bird, the flower, and the gazelle. Enormously bored, wrapped up in his colossal cloak, he slumbers at the edge of his puddle like a drunk near his empty glass.

A pneumatic ox, he dreams that he grazes once again in the submerged meadows of some backwater, or that his tons float placidly among snowy water lilies. From time to time he twitches and snorts, then falls back into the catatonia of his stupor. If he yawns, his malformed mandibles seem to yearn after, to engulf, vast stretches of time gone by.

What is to become of the hippopotamus if he may now serve only as a dredger, a bulldozer of swampy terrain, a paperweight of history? With that great mass of primordial clay one feels like modeling a cloud of birds, an army of mice deployed through the forest, or two or three medium-sized, domestic, acceptable beasts.

But no. The hippopotamus persists just as he is and so reproduces himself: beside the hypnotic tenderness of the female reposes the pink and monstrous baby.

Let us speak of the hippopotamus' tail, amiable, almost smiling item that offers itself to us as the only possible thing to seize onto. Short, thick, smooth, it hangs like a door knocker, like the clapper to the vast bell of his body. It is adorned with a fine fringe of hair along the sides, like a sumptuous tassel between the double curtain of his round, majestic buttocks.

The Zebra

The zebra takes its showy looks seriously, and when it realizes that it is striped, becomes tigerish.

Enclosed in its lustrous lattice, the zebra lives in the galloping captivity of a poorly understood freedom: *Non serviam*, its indomitable nature proudly declares. Abandoning all attempts to tame it, man tried to conquer the zebra's unruliness by submitting it to vile crossbreeding experiments with donkeys and horses. All in vain. Neither stripe nor churlish nature has been eliminated in zebrinos or zebrulas.

Along with the onager and the quagga, the zebra takes pleasure in invalidating man's domination of the equine order. How many brothers of the dog have remained forever untamed, in the role of wolf, coyote, or protelo?

Let us limit ourselves, then, to contemplating the zebra. No other creature has carried to such extremes the possibility of filling out a skin so satisfactorily. The zebras greedily devour African grasslands, knowing full well that neither Arab steed nor thoroughbred can boast a similar sleek roundness of haunch or a like trimness of hoof, nose, and mane. Only the *Przewalski* horse,

surviving model of rupestrian art, is somewhat reminiscent of the zebra's formal stance.

Not satisfied with their clearly special distinction, zebras still indulge their unlimited taste for individual variants, and not a single one has the same stripes as another. Anonymous and solipeds, they display the enormous digital mark that distinguishes them: all zebra-striped, but each in its own fashion.

It is true that many zebras will agree to take two or three turns around the children's circus track. But it is no less true that, faithful to the spirit of their species, they do it obeying a principle of haughty ostentation.

The Giraffe

When God realized he had placed the fruits of a favorite tree too high, he could do nothing but make the giraffe's neck longer.

Quadrupeds with their heads in the air, the giraffes tried to go beyond their corporal reality and resolutely entered the reign of excessive proportions. Problems that seemed to be more engineering and mechanical than biological had to be resolved for them: a nervous system twelve meters long; blood rising against the law of gravity by means of a heart functioning like a deep-well pump; and at such heights, a retractile tongue extending still higher, exceeding by twenty centimeters where the lips can reach to rasp at tree buds like a steel file.

With all its technical extravagance, which extraordinarily complicates it gallop and love-making, the giraffe embodies better than any other creature the madness of the spirit: it seeks in heights what others find right on the ground.

But since now and then it must bend over to drink the common water, it is obliged to unwind its acrobatics in reverse. Then it is down on the burro's level.

The Hyena

An animal requiring few words. The hyena should be described rapidly, almost cursorily. A trio of phrases will do it: howls, repellent odors, somber spots. The limner boggles and sketches only with difficulty the gross mastiff head, the hints of pig and degenerate tiger, the sloping line of the body, slippery, muscular, dwindling.

One moment. We must also record some of the criminal's essential traits: the hyena runs in packs, his snout bristling with fangs, and waylays solitary beasts, always in deserted places. His spasmodic howl is precisely the nocturnal shriek of laughter that disturbs the madhouse. Depraved and gluttonous, he loves the strong flavor of putrefying flesh. To assure himself of a sequence of amorous triumphs, he carries a festering bag of musk between his legs.

Before abandoning this loathsome Cerberus in his ferocious domain, this avid and craven necrophile, we must make a necessary clarification: the hyena has admirers; his propaganda campaign has not been fruitless. He is perhaps the animal that has made the most converts among men.

Deer

Beyond space and time deer roam about with swift slowness, and nobody knows whether they belong in immobility or in movement which they combine to such a degree that we are obliged to place them in eternity.

Inert or dynamic, they constantly modify their natural setting and perfect our ideas about time, space, and moving things. Purposely made to solve the ancient paradox, they are, at once,

Achilles and the tortoise, the bow and the arrow: they run but never reach their goal; they stop and something beyond them always keeps springing.

Unable to remain still, the deer again advances toward us like an apparition, whether from the royal forests or from a legendary wood: St. Hubert's stag bearing a cross on his antlers or the doe that suckled Genevieve of Brabant. Wherever they are found, buck and doe make up the same fabulous pair.

We all try to acquire this hunting piece par excellence, if only by our stare. And if Juan de Yepes tells us that he was so very tall that he overtook his prey, clearly he is not referring to the earthbound dove, but to the profound, fleet, unattainable deer.

The Seals

Laboriously posturing on his muscular flabbiness, one seal raises aloft his altogether naked torso. Another dozes in the sun like a winebag full of heavy water. All the others ply round and round the tank, appearing and disappearing, rolling in the wash caused by their revolutions.

I watch the incessant work of the seals. I hear their jubilant barks, their impudent guffaws, their false alarms of shipwreck. A drop of water splashes my mouth.

Swift shuttles, the seals weave and unravel the interminable fabric of their erotic games. Armless, they embrace and slide from one to another, improvising their rounds *ad libitum*. They spank the water with brisk slaps; they applaud themselves in viscous ovations. The pool seems made of gelatin. The water teems with lips and tongues, and the seals submerge and emerge licking their chops.

Like zoöspores in the microscopic drop, they slither through the cool entrails of the virgin water with ciliated movement, while women and children innocently watch the genetic pantomime.

Mutilated dogs, wingless doves. Ponderous rubber slugs that swim and gallop with difficult ambulacrum. Mere sexual objects. Gigantic microbes. Animate creatures poured into a clay of primary form, potentially fish, reptile, bird, quadruped. Whichever they are, they strike me as gray ovals of soap exuding an intense, repulsive odor.

But what shall we say of their trained sisters, the circus seals that balance crystal balls on the points of their noses, leap like knights on the chessboard, or blow on a row of pipes the first measures of *The Passion According to St. Matthew?*

Water Birds

On the water and the shore the water birds promenade: silly women arrogantly preening in their ridiculous dress. They all belong to high fashion, with or without stilts, and all are gloved.

The feathers of the swallow duck and the spoonbill shine with jeweled splendor. Scarlet, turquoise, ermine, and gold are lavished in plays of changing colors. Some have all these hues in their raiment, like the banal widgeon or the bronzed cormorant that feeds on small putrefactions and transforms into showy dress its fondness for swamp tidbits.

A multicolored, gibbering group, all cawing and honking, where nobody understands anything. I have seen the huge pelican dispute with the big gander over a bit of straw. I have heard the geese gaggle in an interminable argument over nothing, while their eggs roll to the ground and rot in the sun without one of them taking the trouble to hatch them. Males and females come and go through the salon, making bets on who will cross it with

the best waddle. Waterproofed to the nth degree, they are ignorant of the reality of the water in which they live.

The swans traverse the pool with the ostentatious vulgarity of clichés, alluding to the night and the full moon under the midday sun. Their metaphoric neck is always repeating the same plastic refrain— At least there is one black swan that distinguishes itself, drifting along near the shore, bearing in a basket of feathers the serpent of its sleeping neck.

Among all this flock let us make an exception of the heron, submerging in the mud only one foot, which it raises with the effort of an exemplary palafitte. At times the heron huddles down and slumbers under its cover of light feathers, painted one by one by the scrupulously exact Japanese who are so fond of details. It is untempted by an inferior heaven where a bed of clay and rotted matter awaits it.

Monkeys

Wolfgang Köhler wasted five years in Tetuan trying to make a chimpanzee think. Like a good German, he planned a series of mental tricks, obliging the monkey to find his way out of complicated labyrinths and attain difficult tidbits by using ladders, doors, perches, and canes. After such training, Momo became the most intelligent simian in the world; but faithful to his species, he took advantage of all the psychologist's moments of inattention and obtained his rations without crossing the threshold of conscience. He was offered his freedom, but he preferred to stay in his cage.

Now many milennia before (how many?) monkeys decided their fate; they did not give in to the temptation to become men. They did not fall into the rational design and they are still in paradise, caricaturesque, obscene, and free in their manner. In the zoo

now we look at them as at a depressing mirror. They look at us with sarcasm and uneasiness because we keep on watching their animal conduct.

Bound to an invisible dependence, we dance to the music played for us, like the organ grinder's monkey. We seek unsuccessfully a way out of the labyrinths into which we fall, and our minds fail to capture unattainable metaphysical fruits.

The extended interview between Momo and Wolfgang Köhler has cancelled forever all hope of understanding between the primates and ended in another melancholy farewell smacking of failure.

(*Homo sapiens* went to a German university to edit the celebrated treatise on the intelligence of the anthropoids, which gave him fame and fortune, while Momo stayed on in Tetuan enjoying a life pension of fruits within hand's reach.)

The Axolotl

Concerning the axolotl, or mud puppy, I have only two authorities handy that are trustworthy: one, Sahagún, author of *Things of New Spain*; the other, the author of my days.

"Simillima mulierbus!" thus exclaimed the observant Father when he examined thoroughly similar parts in the little body of this siren of Mexican ponds.

A small lizard of jelly. A large waterworm with smooth flat tail and ears of coral polyp. With beautiful ruby eyes, the axolotl is a transparently genital *lingam*. So much so, that women should not bathe in waters where these imperceptible, shiny creatures glide about without taking precautions. (In a town near ours my mother treated a woman who was mortally impregnated with axolotls.)

To get back to Bernardino de Sahagún: ". . . . and its flesh is more delicate than capon's and may be eaten when abstaining from meat. But it can upset the body juices and is bad for continence. The old folks who ate roast axolotls told me that these fish came from an important lady who was having her period, and that a señor from another town had taken her by force, that she did not want to have a child by him, so she douched herself in the lagoon called Axolitla, and that is where the axolotls come from."

I need only add that Nemilov and Jean Rostand are in agreement, pointing out that the female axolotl is one of four animals that suffer the cycle of more or less menstrual biological catastrophes. The other three are the female bat, women, and a certain anthropoid monkey.

PROSODY

Alarm for the Year 2000

Watch out! Every man is a bomb about to explode. Perhaps the beloved will explode in her lover's arms. Perhaps—

Nobody can be pursued or apprehended any more. Everyone refuses to fight. In the earth's most remote corners the noise of the last unhappy mortals resounds.

The marrow of our bones is duly saturated. Each femur and phalanx is an explosive capsule operating at will. All you have to do is rest the tongue firmly against the palatal arch and make a brief angry reflection—5, 4, 3, 2, 1—the adrenalin index increases, the chemistry of the blood is modified, and—boom! Everything around disappears.

Afterwards a light rain of ashes falls. Small viscous clots float in the air. Spiderweb fragments with a faintly nauseating odor like bromine: that is all that remains of man.

There is nothing to do but love each other passionately.

Homage to Otto Weininger

(With a biological reference from
Baron Jakob von Uexküll)

Mange is unbearable in the rays of the sun. I'll stay here in the shade at the foot of this crumbling wall.

Like a good romantic, I wasted my life pursuing a bitch. Hot with excitement, I followed her. She wove labyrinths that led nowhere, not even to the blind alley where I dreamed of catching up with her. Even today, my nose scabby with mange, I reconstructed one of those absurd itineraries which she took, leaving her perfumed visiting cards here and there.

I haven't seen her again. I'm almost blind from rheumy eyes.

But every now and then malicious creatures come to tell me that she is wandering about in this or that district, happily overturning garbage cans and rapturously mating with huge dogs, much bigger than herself.

Then I become rabid, want to bite the first thing that goes by, and give myself up to the health brigade. Or throw myself in the middle of the street to be run over. (Some nights I howl to the moon as a mere formality.)

I'm still here, all mangy, with my sandpaper back. At the foot of this wall where I am slowly digging in the fresh earth. Scratching and scratching myself—

Post Scriptum

With the pistol barrel in my mouth, resting against my palate, with its oily, cold, gun-metal flavor, I felt the strong wave of nausea that all clichés produce in me. "Nobody—"

Don't worry. I'm not going to mention your name here, you who are responsible for my death. The melancholy death you dealt me a year ago, which I lucidly postponed so as not to die like a madman. Do you recall? You left me alone. A knocked-out boxer in his corner with his head in a bucket full of ice.

It is true. Under the blow I felt myself disfigured, confused, indefinable. I still see myself staggering, crossing the street to the opposite post with the extinguished cigarette stuck in my mouth.

I arrived home drunk and sick to my stomach. Face down in the washbasin, I lifted my head and looked at myself in the mirror. My face was like an El Greco, one of his fools from Toledo. I did not want to die looking like that. Destroying the mask took me a whole year. I have regained my features, one by one, posing for death's chisel.

Some condemned men are saved in the death house. I seem to be one of them. But I shall not escape. I enjoy the postponement in the proper style, and here I am, still alive, blocked by a phrase: "nobody is to blame—"

Telemaquia

Wherever there is a duel I shall be on the side of the man who falls, hero or villain.

I am tied by the neck to the theory of slaves sculptured in the most ancient stele. I am the dying warrior beneath Hasurbanipal's chariot, the charred bone in the Dachau ovens.

Hector and Menelaus, France and Germany, and the two drunks breaking each other's noses in the tavern oppress me with their discord. Wherever I turn my eyes an immense tapestry with the face of Good getting the worst of it covers the world's landscape.

An involuntary spectator, I see the contenders start fighting and I don't want to be on anybody's side. Because I am both the one who strikes and the one who receives the blows. Man against man. Does anyone wish to make a bet?

Ladies and gentlemen: There is no salvation. We are losing the match. The Devil is now playing with the white pieces.

Inferno V

Late at night I suddenly awakened at the brink of an abnormal chasm. On the edge of my bed a geological fault cut in somber stone plunged in semicircles, faintly outlined by a tenuous nauseating steam and the wheeling movement of dark birds. Standing on its cornice of slag, almost suspended in the vertigo, was a ridiculous person crowned with laurel who stretched out his hand inviting me to descend.

I politely refused, filled with the terror of night, saying that all expeditions delving into mankind always end up in vain and superficial drivel.

I preferred to put on my light and let myself fall again into the profound monotony of the tercets, where a voice, weeping and talking at the same time, repeats to me that there is no greater sorrow than remembering happy times in misery.

Allons voir si la rose . . .

To the war cry "From now on let us pluck life's roses!" Pierre de Ronsard razed the gardens of France in the second half of the sixteenth century, deflowering the banks of the Loire and the Cher of *mignonnes* and *mignonnettes*.

His fame as a poet has dimmed the prestige he enjoyed during his time in loosening and unfastening bodices, girdles, and skirts with the utmost skill. In reality, he was the best collector around of live roses, the meticulous strolling herbalist of country lanes, the rhetorical trader who swapped sonnets and madrigals for maidenheads in flower.

When the contrast of the faded rose with the peasant girl's cheek didn't work, he would take out his imitation skull and lurk in the shade of the myrtles, lamenting like a premature ghost in order to frighten with the ravages of old age the ingenuous twilight girls.

Let us congratulate Ronsard then for the most modest of his virtues: having hit upon the remarkable metaphor that neatly assured his victory over time. All yesterday's roses become dust in rural cemeteries under this common inscription: "When I was fair, Ronsard sang my praises." *Requiescat in pace!*

The Language of Cervantes

Perhaps I painted his language too much in the style of Fra Angelico. Perhaps I gave excessive attention to the local color of paradise. Perhaps without wishing to I gave out the clue among the catalogue of its virtues, while we emptied mugs of beer and downed hunks of ham and sausage. The truth is that my friend suddenly found the key, the expression, pure, hard, and sharp-edged like a dagger handled by generations of thieves and ruffians, and without further ado, he stabbed me—whore!—in my sentimental heart, whisking the dirty word away with a twirl of his toreador's red cape: the hearty Spanish guffaw that made his leather belt snap before the monumental heave of his Sancho Panza belly, which I had never noticed before.

The Trap

> There is a bird flying
> in search of its cage.
> F. Kafka

Every time a woman approaches, excited and committed, my body quivers with joy and my soul is stricken with horror.

I watch women opening and closing. Thornless roses or carnivorous flowers, in their petals grasping hinges operate: tender eyelids, smoothly oiled with a narcotic. (Round about them buzz the swarm of young pedantic horseflies.)

I get caught in fly-paper souls, sticky as pools of syrup. (An expert at such accidents, I unstick my dragonfly feet one by one. But the last time I wound up with a broken backbone.) And here I go flying alone.

Untruthful sibyls, women are like spiders enmeshed in webs of their own making. And I go on flying alone, fatally, in search of new oracles.

Oh cursed woman, give refuge forever to the cry of my fleeting spirit in the well of your silent flesh!

Disarmed Gentleman

I could not get such ideas out of my head. But one day when I turned a corner, meeting my friend the archangel, he didn't even give me time to greet him, but grabbed me by the horns, and lifting me from the ground with the sincerity of an athlete, made me twirl like a ram in the air. The horns broke right off at the forehead *(tour de force magnifique)* and I fell face down, blinded by the double hemorrhage. Before losing consciousness I made a gesture of gratitude toward my friend, who was escaping on the run while shouting excuses at me.

The healing process was slow and painful, though I tried to speed it up by washing the wounds daily with a little caustic soda dissolved in the waters of Lethe.

Today I saw the archangel again on the occasion of my fortieth birthday. With an exquisite gesture, he brought me my horns as a present, mounted now on a lovely velvet head. Instinctively, I placed them at the foot of my bed as a practical, functional symbol: before going to bed tonight, I hung all my youthful finery on them.

From *L'osservatore*

At the beginning of our era St. Peter's keys were lost in the outskirts of the Roman Empire. Whoever finds them is asked to please
return them to the reigning Pope, since for more than fifteen centuries nobody has been able to force the gates of the Kingdom of
Heaven with picklocks.

Either Or

I too have fought with the angel. Unfortunately for me, the angel
was a strong, mature, and repulsive person wearing a boxer's robe.

Shortly before, we had been vomiting in the bathroom, each one
on his side. Because the banquet, or rather the spree, was of the
worst kind. At home my family—a remote past—was waiting
for me.

Immediately after his proposition, the man began to strangle
me in a determined fashion. The fight, rather the defense, developed like a swift and multiple reflexive analysis for me. I calcu-
lated in an instant all the possibilities of lost salvation, betting on
life or sleep, divided between giving in and dying or postponing
the result of that metaphysical and muscular operation.

Finally I unraveled myself from the nightmare like the magician
who unwinds his mummy bindings and comes out of the locked
coffin. But I still bear on my neck the mortal marks the hands of
my rival left on me, and on my conscience, the certainty that I am
only enjoying a truce, the remorse of having won a banal episode
in the battle that I have irreparably lost.

Achtung! Lebende Tiere!

Once there was a tiny little girl who got into lots of mischief at the zoo. She would get in the cages of sleeping beasts and pull their tails. The brusk awakening of these ferocious animals was all that saved her as she scampered away, escaping.

But one day the little girl came across a gaunt, solitary lion who had lost his former prestige and paid no attention to her. The child abandoned tail pulling and tried stronger measures. She began to tickle the sleeping lion and stirred up one by one all the ideas in his mane. When, with a total lack of reflexes, he failed to respond, she proclaimed herself a lion tamer in a loud voice. The beast then gently turned his head and gobbled her up in one bite.

The zoo officials had a bad time of it because it came out in all the newspapers. The commentators yelled bloody murder and criticized the laws of the universe which allow hungry lions to exist next to incompatible, poorly trained little girls.

Liberty

Today I proclaimed the independence of my acts. Only a few unsatisfied desires and two or three worn-out attitudes gathered together at this ceremony. A grandiose proposal that had offered to come sent its humble excuses at the last minute. All took place in a frightful silence.

I believe the error consisted in its noisy proclamation: trumpets and bells, firecrackers and drums. And to finish off, some ingenious pyrotechnical stunts concerning morality which burned only halfway through.

Finally I found myself alone at midnight, stripped of all my qualities of leadership, performing the job of a mere scribe. With

the last dregs of heroism I undertook the painful task of compos-
ing the articles of a tardy constitution which I shall present to the
general assembly tomorrow. This work amused me a bit, chasing
from my spirit the sad impression of failure.

Light and insidious thoughts of rebellion flutter like butterflies
about the lamp, while over the ruins of my legal prose from time
to time passes a thin strain of the Marseillaise.

The Encounter

Two points attracting each other do not necessarily have to choose
the straight line. Of course, it is the shortest procedure. But there
are some who prefer the infinite.

People fall in each other's arms without skirmishing or pre-
amble. At the most, they advance in a zigzag fashion. Once at
their goal, however, they make up for the detours and mate. Such
brusque love is a shock, and those who strike head on in this way
rebound with a backfire effect. Still propelled willy-nilly like bullets, back through the barrel of the gun they go right into the cartridge case, now empty of powder.

Now and then a pair deviates from this invariable rule. Their
purpose is frankly lineal and not lacking in rectitude. Mysteriously, they decide in favor of the labyrinth. They can not live separated. This is their one certainty, and they are going to lose it
searching for one another. When one of them makes a mistake and
provokes the encounter, the other pretends not to understand and
passes by without a greeting.

The Last Wish

To Giovanni Papini, expert in balance sheets, liquidation sales, and tallying up cash-register receipts, we owe a recent scrutiny of human conscience that balances out more or less equally: *Guidizio Universale*, Florence, 1957.

In circles where he was intimately known they have spread the rumor that he was favored during the last years of his life with supernatural trances, which included blissful visions and tourist trips through heaven and hell.

The wagging, evil tongues say that Papini interviewed our first parents in the uppermost garret of the universe. Adam and Eve, still flesh and blood, have aged prodigiously and remember nothing. It is said that their only remaining illusion is that the Final Judgment and Resurrection of the flesh will soon occur, so they can die no later than the following day and be buried in their native land. Of course, they want a family photograph taken first with all their descendants gathered in the Valley of Josaphat.

We should not be surprised that the editors and biographers of the illustrious Italian storyteller have agreed to omit this moving and childish anecdote from their books.

Imaginary Woman

An imaginary woman you have conjured up is what you want. No consent or courting is necessary. Just now and then an attentive and burning contemplation.

Take a homogenous and dazzling mass, any woman whatsoever (preferably young and beautiful), and lodge her in your head. Don't listen to her talk. In any case, she translates the noises from her mouth into a cabalistic language where absurdity and nonsense become adjusted to the melody of the spheres.

If in the most acute hours of your solitary re-creation the collaboration of her person seems absolutely essential, don't give in. Her imperious memory will lead you amiably by the hand to one of those infantile corners where her condescending and tremulous phantom awaits you, slyly smiling.

Epithalamium

The lovers left their room in a mess, all filled with the residue of their love-making. Garments and faded petals, wine dregs and spilled perfume. Over the rumpled bed, above the deep indentation in the pillow, float words thicker and more charged than aloe and incense, like a cloud of flies. The air is filled with "I love you's" and "My sweet dove."

While I clean and tidy up the bedroom, the morning breeze airs out with its light tongue heavy masses of caramel. Without realizing it, I step on the rosebud she was wearing between her breasts. I seem to hear her now, finicky maiden swooning with love, begging to be petted and caressed. But other days will come when she is left in the nest alone, while her lover goes searching for novelty under other eaves.

I know him. Not long ago he attacked me in the woods, when I was only fifteen. Without any fine phrases or beating about the bush he threw me to the ground and took me. Just like a jolly woodcutter passing by, singing an obscene song, who fells the slender trunk of the young palm tree with one blow.

Elegy

Those vague scars you can see over there in the plowed fields are the ruins of Nobilior's camp. Further on the military fortresses of Castillejo, Renieblas, and Peña Redonda rise up. Of the remote city only one hill, charged with silence, has remained. Near it, bordering it, is that ruin of a river. The Merdancho hums its troubadour's song, and only in the swollen run-offs of June does it resound with epic grandeur.

This peaceful plain witnessed the parade of inept generals: Nobilior, Lepidus, Furio Filo, Caius Hostilius Mancino— Among them, the poet Lucilius, who marched by here with a conqueror's air and returned to Rome battered and dejected, his sword and lyre fallen, the fine point of his epigram blunted.

Legions and legions crashed against the invincible walls. Thousands of soldiers fell before arrows and winter, and in despair. Until one day exasperated Scipion rose up on the horizon like a vengeful wave, and without letting go for months, squeezed with his stubborn hands Numancia's tough neck.

A Theory on Dulcinea

In a lonely place whose name doesn't matter there was once a man who spent his life evading women in their concrete form. He preferred the manual pleasure of reading, and he congratulated himself each time that a knight errant rigorously attacked one of those vague feminine phantoms, all virtues and petticoats, who await the hero after four hundred pages of derring-do, lies, and absurdities.

On the threshold of old age, the anchorite was besieged in his cave by a woman of flesh and blood. She entered his room on any pretext, permeating it with the strong odor of sweat and wool of a country wench who has been out in the sun.

The gentleman lost his head, but far from trapping the woman before him, for pages and pages he pursued a pompous figment of his imagination. He journeyed many leagues, thrust his lance at sheep and windmills, stripped the foliage from a number of oaks, and leaped three or four times in the air. On his return from this fruitless search death was awaiting him at the door of his house. He barely had time to dictate a cavernous will from the depths of his dried-up soul.

But a dusty shepherdess' face was washed with real tears, and for a moment she was transfigured before the demented knight's tomb.

Metamorphosis

Like a meteor capable of shining with its own light at midday, like a small jewel that suddenly contradicts all the flies on earth that have fallen in a plate of soup, the butterfly entered through the window and flew directly into the pot of lentils, where it was shipwrecked.

Dazzled by its instantaneous brilliance (quickly dispersed on the greasy surface of the meal), the man stopped eating and immediately began to restore the wondrous creature. With maniacal patience he gathered one by one the scales of that infinitesimal tiled head, he reconstructed from memory the outline of the outer and inner wings, giving back their primitive grace to the antennae and little feet, emptying and refilling the abdomen until he obtained the wasplike waist that separates it from the thorax, carefully eliminating from each precious particle stains, humidity, and the tiniest blobs of grease.

The soup and his conjugal life grew very cold. At the end of this task, which consumed the best years of his life, the man learned with anguish that he had reconstructed an example of a common butterfly, an *Aphrodita Vulgaris Maculata*, which are found by the thousands in all their mutations and variants, stuck with pins, in the dustiest museums of natural history and in the hearts of all men.

Flower of Ancient Rhetoric

Góngora sending to the nuns a plate of tripe decked with flowers: "from the calves slaughtered / by Don Alonso de Guzmán . . ."

Undoubtedly Don Luis first thought of the end of his poem, which refers to fruitful or barren bellies. Since only virginal entrails can enter nunneries, the poet rejected apples and pears and added a large quantity of flowers to his pedestrian gift.

The tripe on a tray and the flowers in a vase? Not at all. Góngora presented the roses and the tripe together, ingeniously playing with their distinct odors and nuances, carried away by his lyricism to a sincere but problematical position defined by a metaphor-prone churchman.

Flash

London, November 26 (AP). A crazy wise man, whose name has not been revealed, last night placed an Absorber the size of a mousetrap at a tunnel entrance. People waited in vain at the station where the train was supposed to arrive. Men of science are disturbed about this dramatic object that weighs no more than it did before and that has walled in all the cars of the Dover Express and the large number of victims.

To the general consternation, Parliament has declared that the Absorber is in an experimental stage. It consists of a hydrogen capsule in which an atomic vacuum is effected. Originally it was planned by Sir Acheson Beal as a peaceful weapon, destined to annul the effects of nuclear explosions.

The Diamond

Once there was a diamond in the craw of a sadly feathered hen. It fulfilled its mission as a millstone with resigned humility. Some ordinary stones and two or three glass beads accompanied it.

Soon it got a bad reputation because of its hardness. The stones and the glass beads carefully avoided contact with it. The hen enjoyed an admirable digestion as the facets of the diamond ground her food to perfection. Ever more clean and polished, the diamond rolled about in that spasmodic sac.

One day the sadly feathered hen's neck was wrung. Filled with hope, the diamond emerged into the light and began to shine with all the fire of its inner being. But the scullery maid who was cleaning the hen let the diamond with all its reflections run down the drain, filmed with slime.

Honeymoon

She sank first. I must not blame her, for the edges of the moon seemed far away and imprecise, disfigured by the yellow dusk. I went after her, worse luck, and soon we both found ourselves engulfed in the profound sweetness.

Immersed in the thick sea of swimming couples, we navigated

a long time without direction or finding a way out. We floated haphazardly in a torpid embrace, sluggishly making our way through the spherical, never-ending bedroom of honey. Now and then we came across a splinter of reality, an illusory island, a more or less crystallized sugar dome. But that didn't last long. She always found a way to lose her balance, dragging me down again in her fall into the sucking sea.

Realizing that the way out did not lie on the surface, I let myself plumb to the bottom during one of these accidents. There is no telling how long the cloying, vertical descent took. Finally I reached virgin ground. The honey was deposited there in hard, uneven, quartz formations. I began walking, finding a path among the dangerous stalactites. When I got to the open air, I started running like a fugitive. I stopped at a river bank, gulped in deep breaths of air, and washed from my body the last residue of honey.

Only then did I realize that I had lost my companion.

The Map of Lost Objects

The man who sold me the map was not the least bit odd. Just an ordinary-type fellow, perhaps a little sick. He simply accosted me like those vendors you meet on the street. He asked very little money for his map; he wanted to get rid of it at any cost. When he offered to give me a demonstration I accepted out of curiosity, because it was Sunday and I didn't have anything else to do. We went to a nearby spot to look for the sad object that perhaps he himself had thrown there, sure that nobody would pick it up: a rose-colored, celluloid comb, studded with lots of little stones. I still keep it among a dozen such trinkets, and I am especially fond of it because it was the first link in the chain. I regret that I have not kept along with it the other things I sold and the coins I spent. Since that time I have been living off of whatever I find through the map. Quite a wretched life, true, but it has freed me forever from all worry. Fortunately, now and then a lost woman, who mysteriously adjusts herself to my modest means, appears on the map.

Mad with Love

with homage to
Garci-Sánchez de Badajoz

There goes Garci-Sánchez de Badajoz through the deserted garden, early in the morning, exhausted from his all-night amorous vigil, weighted down by his outlandish zither.

Having escaped from his wandering jail, he roams about in the garden of dreams, mad with love, searching under the lilies for the aqueduct's trap door—never mind the world or reason—rolling in the cast of two dark, ferocious, indifferent eyes, falling in the hollow of a bottomless ear.

He covers his corpse of a man scorned with trowelfuls of sad verses, and a nightingale sings for him icy exequies of oblivion. Consoling tears work no marvels; his eyes are dry, clogged with burning salt on the last night of his amorous winter. *For 'twas not love that killed me, / but only the sadness of it.*

Though dying with love, you will not die completely. Something keeps sounding in the shadow of your romantic garden. Look, here is a note of your sad love song which went unheeded. The birds still sing in the branches of your funeral laurel, oh sacrilegious and demented lover.

Because before he reached the paradise of his madness, Garci-Sánchez descended to the lovers' hell. And he heard and said things that scandalized pusillanimous ears, and in a secret letter his verses reached the mailboxes of the somber tribunal.

Gravity

Abysses attract. I live on the edge of your soul. Bent toward you, I fathom your thoughts, I investigate the origin of your acts. Vague desires stir about in the depths, confused and undulating in their reptilian bed.

What does my voracious contemplation feed on? I see the abyss and you are lying in the depths of yourself. No revelation. Nothing that resembles the brusk awakening of conscience. Nothing save the eye that implacably returns my gaze.

A repulsive Narcissus, I contemplate my soul in the bottom of a well. Sometimes dizziness turns my eyes from you. But I always go back to scrutinizing the depths. Others who are happy look at your soul for a moment and then leave.

I continue at the edge, wrapped up in myself. Many beings plummet in the distance. Their remains lie blurred, dissolved in satisfaction. Attracted by the abyss, I live with the melancholy certainty that I am never going to fall.

The Cave

Nothing but horror, pure and empty space. That is Tribenciano's cave. A stony hollow in the bowels of the earth. A long rounded cavity like an egg. Two hundred meters long and eighty wide. Cupolas everywhere, of smooth jasper stone.

Seventy steps, in flights of unequal length, descend to the cavern through a natural crack which opens like a simple block on the surface of the ground. What does one descend to? Death. All over the floor of the cave there are bones and lots of dust from bones. We don't know whether people descended on their own initiative or whether they were sent there by special order. Whose?

Some investigators think that the cave does not contain a cruel mystery. They say it is just an ancient cemetery, perhaps Etruscan, perhaps Ligurian. But nobody can stay in it more than five minutes without running the risk of losing consciousness. Scientists try to explain why those who venture into it faint by saying that subterranean emanations of gas surface in the cave. But nobody knows what gas it is nor where it comes from. Perhaps what attacks man there is his horror of pure space, nothingness in its concave silence.

That is all we know about Tribenciano's cave. Thousands of cubic meters of nothing in its round autoclave. Nothing in a stone shell. Smooth jasper stone. With the dust of death.

Others' Possessions

There is nothing more deplorable and pitiful, thieves say, than the gesture of a man surprised in the flagrant crime of property. He trembles, stammers, heavily lifts his hands and waves them in the air as if they were empty. Finally, he says that he has nothing, that it is all a lie, that it is undoubtedly a lamentable mistake.

In reality it is very difficult to recognize one's own errors, and nobody willingly gives away what belongs to him. Thieves, always on the point of showing weakness, tighten their hearts and end by taking something against the owner's will. Those who try to rob without a pistol run very grave risks, since proprietors abuse them and are wont to take the offensive. Frequently the newspaper gives an account of some imprudent and harmless fellow who was riddled with bullets while making his escape empty-handed.

Nonetheless, say the thieves, from time to time they manage to find some repentant souls who give back everything they have on them, solemnly welcoming the nocturnal visit as an act of providence.

CONFABULARIO

. . . mudo espío
mientras alguien voraz a mí me observa.
Carlos Pellicer

Parturient Montes

". . . nascetur ridiculus mus."
Horace, *Ad Pisones*, 139.

Among friends and enemies the word got around that I knew a fresh version of the birth of the mountains. They have asked me to tell it everywhere, giving signs of an eager anticipation which far exceeds the interest of such a tale. In all honesty I referred my curious public again and again to the classical texts and the fashionable editions. But nobody was content with this; they all wanted to hear it from my lips. Depending on their temperament, they progressed from friendly insistence to threats, violence, and bribery. Some phlegmatic types feigned indifference in order to wound my self-respect to the quick. Direct action had to be employed sooner or later.

Yesterday I was assaulted right on the street by one resentful group. Cutting me off on all sides, they shouted at me to begin telling the story. Many passersby, distracted, stopped too, not knowing they would take part in a crime. Undoubtedly taken in by my compromising charlatan aspect, they willingly added themselves to the throng. I soon found myself surrounded by the compact mass.

Overwhelmed and with no escape, I summoned all my energy and proposed to put an end to my prestige as a narrator. Here is the result. In a voice high-pitched with emotion, standing on a traffic policeman's stool which someone thrust under my feet, I began to declaim the same old words in the usual way: "In the midst of earthquakes and explosions, with majestic rumblings of pain, uprooting trees and tearing out rocks, some gigantic event is imminent. Is a volcano being born? A river of fire? Will a new and submerged star rise on the horizon? Ladies and gentlemen, the mountains are giving birth."

Stupor and shame stifle my words. For several seconds I continue the speech in pure pantomime, like a director before a mute orchestra. My failure is so real and evident that some people are moved. "Bravo!" I hear shouted over there, encouraging me to fill in the lacuna. Instinctively, I put my hands on my head and squeeze it with all my force, wishing to hasten the end of the story. The spectators have guessed that it concerns the legendary mouse, but they pretend to a sick anxiety. Around me I feel a single heart beating.

I know the rules of the game, and deep down I don't like to defraud anyone with a prestidigitator's way out. Suddenly I forget everything. What I learned at school and what I've read in books. My mind is a blank. In good faith I set myself to pursuing the mouse. There is a respectful silence for the first time. A few in the audience relate to newcomers in hushed voices certain antecedents of the drama. I am really in a fix and search everywhere for the way out like a man who has lost his reason.

I go through my pockets one by one and turn them inside out in view of the public. I take off my hat and thrust it aside immediately, rejecting the idea of pulling out a rabbit. I undo the knot in my tie and continue, fumbling with my shirt until my hands stop in horror at the top button of my pants.

When I am just about to faint, a woman's face that suddenly kindles with a hopeful blush saves me. Steadying myself on my pedestal, I place all my hope in her and raise her to the category of muse, forgetting that women have a special weakness for scabrous themes. The tension reaches its maximum point at this moment. Who was the charitable soul who, realizing my predicament, made the phone call? The ambulance siren introduces a definite threat on the horizon.

At the last moment my smile of relief deters those who were undoubtedly thinking of lynching me. Here, under my right arm in the hollow of my armpit, is a slight, nestlike warmth— Something is moving and stirring here— Gently I let my arm fall along my body with my hand cupped like a spoon. And the miracle is produced. Down the tunnel of my sleeve comes a crumb of life. I lift up my arm and extend a triumphal palm.

I sigh and the crowd sighs with me. Unwittingly, I give the signal for applause and the ovation is not long in coming. An astonished line is rapidly formed before the newborn mouse. Those who realize what has happened approach and look it all over, making sure that it breathes and moves; they have never seen anything like it and heartily congratulate me. As soon as they have taken a few steps away, however, their objections start. They doubt, they shrug their shoulders and shake their heads. Was there a trick? Is it really a mouse? To calm me down, some of the more enthusiastic fellows there propose that they carry me on their shoulders, but that is as far as it goes. The audience disperses little by little. Weak from the effort and almost alone now, I am ready to give the creature away to the first person who asks for it.

Women are almost always afraid of these rodents, but the one whose face shone out in the crowd approaches and timidly reclaims the intimate fruit of fantasy. Utterly flattered, I immediately dedicate it to her, and my confusion is complete when she tucks it lovingly in her breast.

As she departs and thanks me, she explains her attitude as best she can, so there won't be any bad interpretations. Seeing her so flustered, I listen enchanted. She has a cat, she says, and she lives with her husband in a deluxe apartment. She is simply planning to give them a little surprise. Nobody knows there what a mouse is.

I'm Telling You the Truth

Everybody who is interested in seeing the camel pass through the eye of the needle should inscribe his name on the list of patrons for the Niklaus Experiment.

Disassociated from a group of death-dealing scientists, the kind who manipulate uranium, cobalt, and hydrogen, Arpad Niklaus is guiding his present research toward a charitable and radically humanitarian end: the salvation of the souls of the rich.

He proposes a scientific plan to disintegrate a camel and make it pass in a stream of electrons through a needle's eye. A receiving apparatus (very similar to the television screen) will organize the electrons into atoms, the atoms into molecules, and the molecules into cells, immediately reconstructing the camel according to its original scheme. Niklaus has already managed to make a drop of heavy water change its position without touching it. He has also been able to evaluate, up to the point where the discretion of the material permits, the quantum energy discharged by a camel's hoof. It seems pointless here to burden the reader with that astronomical figure.

The only serious difficulty Professor Niklaus has run into is the lack of his own atomic plant. Such installations, extensive as cities, are incredibly expensive. But a special committee is already busy solving the problem by means of a world-wide subscription drive. The first contributions, still rather anemic, are serving to defray the cost of thousands of pamphlets, bonds, and explanatory prospectuses, as well as to assure Professor Niklaus the modest salary permitting him to continue with his calculations and theoretical investigations while the immense laboratories are being built.

At present, the committee can count only on the camel and the needle. As the societies for the prevention of cruelty to animals approve the project, which is inoffensive and even healthful for any camel (Niklaus speaks of a probable regeneration of all the cells), the country's zoos have offered a veritable caravan. New York City has not hesitated to risk its very famous white dromedary.

As for the needle, Arpad Niklaus is very proud of it and considers it the keystone of the experiment. It is not just any needle, but a marvelous object discovered by his assiduous talent. At first glance, it might be confused with a common ordinary needle. Mrs. Niklaus, displaying a fine sense of humor, takes pleasure in mending her husband's clothes with it. But its value is infinite. It is made from an extraordinary, as yet unclassified, metal, whose chemical formula, scarcely hinted at by Niklaus, seems to indicate that it involves a base composed exclusively of isotopes of nickel. This mysterious substance has made scientists ponder a great deal. There was even one who sustained the laughable hypothesis of a synthetic osmium or an abnormal molybdenum, or still another who dared to proclaim in public the words of an envious professor who was sure he had recognized Niklaus' metal in the form of tiny crystalline clusters encysted in dense masses of siderite. What is known with certainty is that Niklaus' needle can resist the friction of a stream of electrons flowing at ultrasonic speed.

In one of those explanations so pleasing to abstruse mathematicians, Professor Niklaus compares the camel in its transit to a spider's thread. He tells us that if we were to use that thread to weave a fabric, we would need all of sidereal space to stretch it out in, and that the visible and invisible stars would be caught in it like sprays of dew. The skein in question measures millions of light years, and Niklaus is offering to wind it up in about three-fifths of a second.

As can be seen, the project is completely viable, and, we might even say, overly scientific. It can already count on the sympathy and moral support (not officially confirmed yet) of the Interplanetary League, presided over in London by the eminent Olaf Stapledon.

In view of the natural expectation and anxiety that Niklaus' project has provoked everywhere, the committee is manifesting a special interest by calling the world powers' attention to it, so they will not let themselves be surprised by charlatans who are passing dead camels through subtle orifices. These individuals, who do not hesitate to call themselves scientists, are simply swindlers on the lookout for imprudent optimists. They proceed by an extremely vulgar method, dissolving the camel in sulphuric acid solutions each time lighter than the last. Then they distil the liquid through the needle's eye, using a steam clepsydra, believing that they have performed the miracle. As one can see, the experiment is useless, and there is no reason to finance it. The camel must be alive before and after the impossible transfer.

Instead of melting down tons of candle wax and spending money on indecipherable works of charity, persons interested in the eternal life who have more capital than they know what to do with should subsidize the disintegration of the camel, which is scientific, colorful, and, ultimately, lucrative. To speak of generosity in such a case is totally unnecessary. One must shut one's eyes and open one's purse generously, knowing full well that all expenses will be met pro rata. The reward for all the contributors will be the same; what is urgent is to hasten the date of payment as much as possible.

The total capital necessary cannot be known until the unpredictable end, and Professor Niklaus, in all honesty, refuses to work with a budget that is not fundamentally elastic. The subscribers should pay out their investment quotas patiently over the years. It is necessary to contract for thousands of technicians, managers, and workers. Regional and national subcommittees must be established. And the statute founding a school of successors for Professor Niklaus must not only be foreseen, but budgeted for in detail, since the experiment might reasonably extend over several generations. In this respect, it is not beside the point to indicate the ripe old age of the learned Niklaus.

Like all human plans, Experiment Niklaus offers two probable results: failure and success. Besides simplifying the problem of personal salvation, a success by Niklaus will convert the promoters of such a mystical experience into stockholders of a fabulous transport company. It will be very easy to develop the disintegration of human beings in a practical and economical way. The men of tomorrow will travel great distances in an instant and without danger, dissolved in electronic flashes.

But the possibility of a failure is even more attractive. If Arpad Niklaus is a maker of chimeras and is followed at his death by a whole line of imposters, his humanitarian work will only have increased in grandeur, like a geometric progression or the texture of a chicken bred by Carrel. Nothing will keep him from passing into history as the glorious innovator of the universal disintegration of capital. And the rich, impoverished en masse by the draining investments, will easily enter the kingdom of heaven by the narrow gate (the eye of the needle), though the camel may not pass through.

Interview

"Finally, our readers would like to know what you are working on now. Could you say?"

"Last night something happened to me, but I don't know, I don't know—"

"Oh, go ahead and say it."

"It has to do with something like a whale. It's the wife of a young poet, let us say of an ordinary, common man."

"Oh, yes! The whale that gobbled up Jonah."

"Yes, yes, but not just Jonah. It's a kind of total whale that has inside it all the fish it has been eating, one by one, of course, always from the largest to the smallest, and beginning with the microscopic infusorian."

"Fine, fine! When I was a child I too thought about such an animal, but I believe that in my case it was a kangaroo in whose pouch—"

"Well, I would really have no objection to changing the image from the whale to the kangaroo. I like kangaroos with their huge pouches which the world could well fit into. Only, you see, since it's about the wife of a young poet, the whale image is much more suggestive. A blue whale, if you prefer, so as not to leave gallantry aside."

"Where did you get such an idea?"

"It's the gift of the poet himself, the whale's husband."

"How's that?"

"In one of his most beautiful poems he conceives of himself as a tiny little fish adhering to the body of the great nocturnal whale, the sleeping wife who guides him in his dreams. That enormous feminine whale is more or less the world, and the poet can only celebrate in song a fragment of it, a bit of that sweet skin that sustains him."

"I'm afraid that your words are going to disconcert our readers and the editor, you know—"

"In that case, give a tranquilizing turn to my ideas. Simply say that the whale has swallowed us all, you and me, the newspaper readers and the editor, that we live in its insides, that it is slowly digesting us and little by little casting us out into the void—"

"Bravo! Say no more. It's perfect, and right in our newspaper's style. Oh, a final question—could you let us have a photograph?"

"No. I prefer to give you a panoramic vista of the whale. We are all there. With a little care you can easily distinguish me—I don't remember exactly where—enveloped in a small, shining light."

The Rhinoceros

For ten years I fought with a rhinoceros; I'm the divorced wife of Judge McBride. Joshua McBride possessed me for ten years with his imperious egoism. I knew his furious rages, his momentary tenderness, and, late at night, his insistent and ceremonious lust.

I renounced love before I knew what it was, because Joshua showed me with judicial allegations that love is just a story good for entertaining servant girls. On the other hand, he offered me his protection as a respectable man. According to Joshua, the protection of a respectable man is the highest ambition of every woman.

Ten years I fought with the rhinoceros, body to body, and my only triumph consisted in dragging him to divorce.

Joshua McBride has remarried, but this time he has made a mistake in his choice. Seeking another Eleanor, he met his match. Pamela is sweet and romantic, but she knows the secret that helps to subdue rhinoceroses. Joshua McBride attacks head on, but can not turn about rapidly. When anyone gets behind him, he has to wheel completely around to attack again. Pamela seizes him by the tail, shakes it, and won't let go. Having to circle around so much, the judge begins to show signs of fatigue, relents, and gives in. His rages have become slower and more melancholy; his harangues, like a disconcerted actor's, no longer are convincing. He is like a subterranean volcano with Pamela sitting on top, smiling. On the seas with Joshua I was shipwrecked; Pamela floats like a little paper boat in a wash basin. She is the daughter of a prudent vegetarian pastor who taught her how to make tigers turn prudent and vegetarian too.

Not long ago I saw Joshua in church devoutly listening to the Sunday services. He seems emaciated and flattened. Just as though Pamela, with her two fragile hands, has been reducing his volume and folding up his spine. His vegetarian pallor gives him a smooth, sickly cast.

People who visit the McBrides tell me surprising things. They speak of incomprehensible meals, lunches and suppers with no roast beef; they describe Joshua devouring enormous platters of salad. Naturally, from such nourishment he can not extract the calories that made his former rages so impressive. His favorite dishes have been methodically altered or suppressed by grim and implacable cooks. Patagras and Gorgonzola cheese no longer permeate the dark oak dining room with their strong odor. They have been replaced by insipid and odorless cream cheeses which Joshua eats in silence, like a punished child. Pamela, ever amiable and smiling, puts out Joshua's half-smoked cigar, rations his pipe tobacco and his whiskey.

That's what they tell me. I like to imagine the two of them alone dining at a long narrow table under the cold light of the candelabra. Watched by the wise Pamela, gluttonous Joshua sullenly munches his light meals. But I especially like to imagine the rhinoceros late at night, in his slippers, his great shapeless body under his robe, knocking timidly and persistently on an obstinate door.

The Bird Spider

The bird spider scuttles freely about the house, but my feeling of horror does not diminish.

The day when Beatrice and I entered that filthy hut in the street market, I realized that the repulsive creature was the most atrocious thing destiny could design for me. Worse than scorn and commiseration suddenly shining clearly in someone's face.

Some days later I returned to buy the bird spider, and the surprised trainer gave me some information about its habits and strange food. Then I understood that I held in my hands, once and for all, the total threat, the maximum terror my spirit could endure. I remember my trembling, vacillating steps when on my return home I felt the spider's light, yet heavy weight in the wooden box I was carrying. It was as if there were two totally different weights involved: the innocent box's and the impure, poisonous animal's, that pulled away from me like real ballast. Within that box was the personal hell that I would install in my house in order to destroy, to annul, the other strange hell—man's.

The memorable night when I let the bird spider loose in my apartment and saw it run like a crab and hide under a piece of furniture was the beginning of an indescribable life. From then on every instant in my life has been attuned to the spider's movements, filling the house with its invisible presence.

Every night I lie trembling, waiting for its mortal bite. I wake up many times, my body tense and motionless, for my dream has created for me in precise detail the spider's tickling movement across my skin, its indefinable weight, its visceral consistency. Nevertheless, each day arrives anew. I am alive and my soul uselessly prepares and perfects itself.

There are days when I think that the bird spider has disappeared, that it has gone away or died. But I do nothing to verify this. I always concede that chance may bring me face to face with it again while stepping out of my bath or undressing for bed. Sometimes the night's silence brings me an echo of its footsteps that I have learned to detect, though I know they are imperceptible.

Many days I find the food I have left the evening before untouched. When it disappears, I don't know whether the bird spider or some other guest in the house has devoured it. I have also come to think that perhaps I am the victim of a trick, that I am at the mercy of a false bird spider. Perhaps the trainer cheated me, making me pay a high price for a harmless and repugnant beetle.

But this really has no importance, because I have consecrated the bird spider with the certainty of my eventual death. During the most acute hours of insomnia, when I lose myself in conjectures and nothing calms me down, the bird spider is wont to visit me. It zigzags confusedly about the room and clumsily tries to climb the walls. It stops, lifts its head and moves its feelers. Excited, it seems to sniff an invisible companion.

Then, shivering in my solitude, cornered by the little monster, I recall that in another time I dreamt of Beatrice and her impossible company.

Figment of a Dream

I lack reality and I'm afraid I don't interest anyone. I am a scoundrel, a dependent, a phantom. I live among fears and desires; life-giving fears and desires that are killing me at the same time. I repeat: I am a scoundrel.

I lie in the shadow in long and incomprehensible periods of oblivion. Suddenly they oblige me to come out into the light, a blinding light that almost assures me reality. But then they busy themselves again with each other and forget me. I am lost again in the shadows, making gestures which become more and more imprecise, reduced to nothingness, to sterility.

Night is my best time. In vain the husband, tortured in his nightmare, tries to push me away. At times I vaguely satisfy the wife's desire with agitation and torpor. Curled up, she defends herself in her dream, but finally surrenders, long and soft as a pillow.

I live a precarious life divided between these two beings who love and hate each other and who produce me like a deformed son. Nonetheless, I am beautiful and terrible. I destroy their tranquility or kindle them with the hottest love. Sometimes I place myself between them and their intimate embrace marvelously enfolds me. He notices my presence and tries to annihilate me and take my place. But finally, exhausted and defeated and devoured by rancor, he turns his back on the woman. Throbbing, I stay next to her, and circling her with my absent arms, little by little I dissolve in the dream.

I should have started out by saying that I have not been born yet, that I am slowly in the form of gestation, suffering in a long and submerged process. Unconsciously, they mistreat my still unborn existence with their love.

They plan my life in their thoughts, clumsy hands that insist on shaping me, giving me form and then taking it away, always dissatisfied.

But one day when perchance they give me my definitive form, I shall escape and be able to dream myself, vibrant with reality. Then they will separate. And I shall abandon the woman and pursue the man. I shall guard the bedroom door brandishing a flaming sword.

A Reputation

Courtesy is not my strong point. When traveling I try to hide this failing by reading or looking dejected. But today I automatically gave up my seat without realizing it to a standing woman who looked vaguely like an announcing angel.

The lady benefiting from that look greeted my action with such effusive words that they attracted the attention of two or three passengers. Soon afterward, the seat next to her became empty, and when she offered it to me with a light and significant gesture, her angelic face registered a beautiful look of relief. I sat down there hoping that the trip would continue without complication.

But that day was mysteriously fatal for me. Another woman without the image of wings got on the bus. A good opportunity arrived for me to clarify the situation, but I didn't take advantage of it. Naturally, I could have remained seated, thus destroying the beginnings of a false reputation. Nonetheless, being weak and feeling myself compromised now with my companion, I hastened to get up, offering my seat with a bow to the recent arrival. It seems that nobody had rendered her such homage in all her life: she went to extremes with her garbled words of gratitude.

This time it wasn't just two or three people who approved of my courtesy with their smiles. At least half the passengers gazed at me, as if saying: "Here is a gentleman." I thought about leaving the vehicle, but I immediately thought better of it, manfully resigning myself to the situation, nourishing the hope that things would go no further.

Two streets further on a passenger got off. From the other end of the bus, a lady pointed out the empty seat to me. She did this with just a glance, but so imperiously that it stopped a man who was getting there ahead of me; at the same time, it was such a sweet glance, that I walked back through the bus with hesitant steps to occupy a place of honor in that seat. Some masculine passengers who were afoot smiled scornfully. I perceived their envy, jealousy, and resentment, and felt rather upset. On the other hand, the women seemed to protect me with their silent, effusive approval.

A new trial that was much more important than the preceding ones awaited me at the following corner: a woman with two little children got on the bus. A little angel in arms and another scarcely able to walk. Obeying the unanimous order, I got up immediately and went to meet that touching group. To complicate things, the lady had two or three packages; she had had to run half a block at least and wasn't able to get her handbag open. I helped her efficiently in every way possible, relieving her of babies and packages, persuading the chauffeur that the children shouldn't have to pay, and the lady was finally installed in my seat that feminine surveillance had kept free from intruders. I held onto the oldest child's hand.

My compromises with the passengers increased in a decisive manner. Everyone expected something from me. At that moment I personified feminine ideals of chivalry and protection of the weak. The responsibility oppressed my body like a heavily weighted armor, and I missed having a good sword at my side. For serious things kept happening to me. For example, if a passenger made passes at some lady, not a rare occurrence on busses, I had to threaten the aggressor and enter into combat with him. In any case, the ladies seemed completely sure of my chivalrous Bayardo reaction. I felt myself teetering on the edge of a drama.

At this moment we arrived at the corner where I should get off. I saw my house—a promised land. But I didn't get off. I couldn't move, and the bus' starting up again gave me some idea of what a transatlantic adventure must be like. I recovered rapidly; I could not desert like this, defrauding those who had pledged their safety to me, entrusting me with the position of command. Besides, I must confess that I felt inhibited by the idea that my getting off the bus would unleash impulses contained until then. If on the one hand I felt sure of what the feminine majority thought of me, I was not very easy about my reputation among the men. When I got off, either applause or whistles might explode at my back. I could not run such a risk. And suppose, taking advantage of my absence, one of the men annoyed with me gave rein to his lower instincts? I decided to stay on and be the last to get off at the terminal when everyone was safe.

One by one the women happily got off at their respective corners. The driver—praise God!—brought the bus close to the curb and to a complete stop, waiting for the women to step off onto terra firma. At the last moment, I saw on each face a friendly look with a faint suggestion of an affectionate goodbye. With my help the woman with the children finally got off, but not without bestowing on me a pair of childish kisses, which still lie heavy on my heart like remorse.

I descended at a lonely, deserted corner without pomp or ceremony. My spirit still held large reserves of unused heroism, while the bus went off into the distance, emptied of that scattered and fortuitous assemblage that had consecrated my reputation as a gentleman.

The Switchman

The stranger arrived at the deserted station out of breath. His large suitcase, which nobody carried for him, had really tired him out. He mopped his face with a handkerchief, and with his hand shading his eyes, gazed at the tracks that melted away in the distance. Dejected and thoughtful, he consulted his watch: it was the exact time when the train was supposed to leave.

Somebody, come from heaven knows where, gently tapped him. When he turned around, the stranger found himself before a little old man who looked vaguely like a railroader. In his hand he was carrying a red lantern, but so small it seemed a toy. Smiling, he looked at the stranger, who anxiously asked him: "Excuse me, but has the train already left?"

"Haven't you been in this country very long?"

"I have to leave right away. I must be in T—— tomorrow at the latest."

"It's plain you don't know what's going on at all. What you should do right now is go look for lodging at the inn," and he pointed to a strange, ash-colored building that looked more like a jail.

"But I don't want lodging; I want to leave on the train."

"Rent a room immediately if there are any left. In case you can get one, take it by the month. It will be cheaper for you and you will get better attention."

"Are you crazy? I must get to T—— by tomorrow."

"Frankly, I ought to leave you to your fate. But just the same, I'll give you some information."

"Please—"

"This country is famous for its railroads, as you know. Up to now it's been impossible to organize them properly, but great progress has been made in publishing timetables and issuing tickets. Railroad guides include and link all the towns in the country; they sell tickets for even the smallest and most remote villages. Now all that is needed is for the trains to follow what the guides indicate and really pass by the stations. The inhabitants of this country hope this will happen; meanwhile, they accept the service's irregularities and their patriotism keeps them from showing any displeasure."

"But is there a train that goes through this city?"

"To say yes would not be accurate. As you can see, the rails exist, though they are in rather bad shape. In some towns they are simply marked on the ground by two chalk lines. Under the present conditions, no train is obliged to pass through here, but nothing keeps that from happening. I've seen lots of trains go by in my life and I've known some travelers who managed to board them. If you wait until the right moment, perhaps I myself will have the honor of helping you get on a nice comfortable coach."

"Will that train take me to T——?"

"Why do you insist that it has to be T——? You should be satisfied if you get on it. Once on the train, your life will indeed take on some direction. What difference does it make, whether it's T—— or not?"

"But my ticket is all in order to go to T——. Logically, I should be taken there, don't you agree?"

"Most people would say you are right. Over at the inn you can talk to people who have taken precautions, acquiring huge quantities of tickets. As a general rule, people with foresight buy pas-

sage to all points of the country. There are some who have spent a real fortune on tickets—"

"I thought that to go to T—— one ticket was enough. Look here—"

"The next stretch of the national railways is going to be built with the money of a single person who has just spent his immense capital on round-trip passages for a railroad track that includes extensive tunnels and bridges that the engineers haven't even approved the plans for."

"But is the train that goes through T—— still in service?"

"Not just that one. Actually, there are a great many trains in the nation, and travelers can use them relatively often, if they take into account that it's not a formal and definitive service. In other words, nobody expects when he gets aboard a train to be taken where he wants to go."

"Why is that?"

"In its eagerness to serve the citizens, the railway management is forced to take desperate measures. They make trains go through impassable places. These expeditionary trains sometimes take several years on a trip and the passengers' lives suffer important transformations. Deaths are not unusual in such cases, but the management, foreseeing everything, hitches on to those trains a car with a funeral chapel and a cemetery coach. The conductors take pride in depositing the traveler's body, luxuriously embalmed, on the station platform prescribed by his ticket. Occasionally these trains are compelled to run on roadbeds where one of the rails is missing. All one side of the coaches shudders lamentably as the wheels hit the railroad ties. The first-class passengers—another instance of the management's foresight—are seated on the side where there is a rail. But there are other stretches where both rails are missing; there all the passengers suffer equally, until the train is completely wrecked."

"Good Lord!"

"Listen, the village of F—— came into being because of one of those accidents. The train found itself in impassable terrain. Smoothed and polished by the sand, the wheels were worn away to their axles. The passengers had spent such a long time together that from the obligatory trivial conversations intimate friendships sprang up. Some of those friendships soon became idylls, and the result is F——, a progressive town filled with mischievous children playing with the rusty vestiges of the train."

"For Heaven's sake, I'm not one for such adventures!"

"You need to pluck up your courage; perhaps you may even become a hero. You must not think there aren't occasions for the passengers to show their courage and capacity for sacrifice. On one occasion two hundred anonymous passengers wrote one of the most glorious pages in our railroad annals. It happened that on a trial journey the engineer noticed in time that the builders of the line had made a grave omission. A bridge that should have spanned an abyss just wasn't there. Well now, the engineer, instead of backing up, gave the passengers a pep talk and got the necessary cooperation from them to continue forward. Under his forceful direction the train was taken apart piece by piece and carried on the passengers' backs to the other side of the abyss, which held a further surprise: a turbulent river at its bottom. The management was so pleased with the results of this action that it definitely renounced the construction of the bridge, only going so far as to make an attractive discount in the fares of those passengers who dared to take on that additional nuisance."

"But I've got to get to T—— tomorrow!"

"All right! I'm glad to see you aren't giving up your project. It's plain that you are a man of conviction. Stay at the inn for the time being and take the first train that comes. At least try to; a thousand people will be there to get in your way. When a train comes in, the travelers, exasperated by an overly long wait, stream tumultuously out of the inn and noisily invade the station. Frequently they cause accidents with their incredible lack of courtesy and prudence. Instead of getting on the train in an orderly fashion, they devote themselves to crushing one another; at least, they keep each other from boarding, and the train goes off leaving them piled up on the station platforms. Exhausted and furious, the travelers curse each other's lack of good breeding and spend a lot of time hitting and insulting each other."

"Don't the police intervene?"

"They tried to organize a police force for each station, but the trains' unpredictable arrivals made such a service useless and very expensive. Besides, the members of the force soon showed their corrupt character, only letting wealthy passengers who gave them everything they had board the trains. Then a special kind of school was established where future travelers receive lessons in etiquette and adequate training so they can spend their lives on the trains. They are taught the correct way to board a train, even though it is moving at great speed. They are also given a kind of armor so the other passengers won't crack their ribs."

"But once on the train, aren't your troubles over?"

"Relatively speaking, yes. But I recommend that you watch the stations very carefully. You might think you had arrived at T——, and it would only be an illusion. In order to regulate life on board the overcrowded coaches, the management has been obliged to take certain expedient measures. There are stations that are for appearance only: they have been built right in the jungle and they bear the name of some important city. But you just need to pay a little attention to see through the deceit. They are like stage sets, and the people on them are stuffed with sawdust. These dummies easily betray the ravages of bad weather, but sometimes they are a perfect image of reality: their faces bear the signs of an infinite weariness."

"Fortunately, T—— isn't very far from here."

"But at the moment we don't have any through trains. Never-

theless, it could well happen that you might arrive at T——
tomorrow, just as you wish. The management of the railroads,
although not very efficient, doesn't exclude the possibility of a
nonstop journey. You know, there are people who haven't even
realized what is going on. They buy a ticket for T——. A train
comes, they get on it, and the next day they hear the conductor
announce: 'We're at T——.' Without making sure, the passengers
get off and find themselves indeed in T——."

"Could I do something to bring about that result?"

"Of course you could. But it's hard to tell if it will do any good.
Try it anyway. Get on the train with the firm idea that you are
going to reach T——. Don't talk with any of the passengers. They
might disillusion you with their travel tales and they might even
denounce you."

"What are you saying?"

"Because of the present state of things the trains are full of
spies. These spies, mostly volunteers, dedicate their lives to
encouraging the company's constructive spirit. Sometimes one
doesn't know what one is saying and talks just to be talking. But
they immediately see all the meanings in a phrase, however simple it may be. They can twist the most innocent comment around
to make it look guilty. If you were to commit the slightest imprudence you would be apprehended without further ado; you
would spend the rest of your life in a prison car, if they didn't
make you get off at a false station, lost out in the jungle. While
you travel, have faith, consume the smallest possible amount of
food, and don't step off onto the platform until you see some fa-
miliar face at T——."

"But I don't know anybody in T——."

"In that case, take double precautions. There will be many temp-
tations on the way, I assure you. If you look out the windows,
you may fall into the trap of a mirage. The train windows are provided with ingenious devices that create all kinds of illusions in

the passengers' minds. You don't have to be weak to fall for them. Certain apparatuses, operated from the engine, make you believe that the train is moving because of the noise and the movements. Nevertheless, the train stands still for whole weeks at a time while the passengers looking through the window panes see captivating landscapes pass by."

"What object is there in that?"

"The management does all this with the wholesome purpose of reducing the passengers' anxiety and, as far as possible, the sensations of moving. The hope is that one day the passengers will capitulate to fate, give themselves into the hands of an omnipotent management, and no longer care to know where they are going or where they have come from."

"And you, have you traveled a lot on trains?"

"Sir, I'm just a switchman. To tell the truth, I'm a retired switchman, and I just come here now and then to remember the good old days. I've never traveled and I have no desire to. But the travelers tell me stories. I know that the trains have created many towns besides F——, whose origin I told you about. Sometimes the crew on a train receives mysterious orders. They invite the passengers to get off, usually on the pretext that they should admire the beauties of a certain place. They are told about grottos, falls, or famous ruins: 'Fifteen minutes to admire such and such a grotto,' the conductor amiably calls out. Once the passengers are a certain distance away, the train chugs away at full speed."

"What about the passengers?"

"They wander about disconcertedly from one spot to another for a while, but they end up by getting together and establishing a colony. These untimely stops occur in places far from civilization but with adequate resources and sufficient natural riches. Selected lots of young people, and especially an abundant number of women, are abandoned there. Wouldn't you like to end your days in a picturesque unknown spot in the company of a young girl?"

The little old fellow winked, and smiling kindly, continued to gaze roguishly at the traveler. At that moment a faint whistle was heard. The switchman jumped, all upset, and began to make ridiculous, wild signals with his lantern.

"Is it the train?" asked the stranger.

The old man recklessly broke into a run along the track. When he had gone a certain distance he turned around to shout, "You are lucky! Tomorrow you will arrive at your famous station. What did you say its name was?"

"X——!" answered the traveler.

At that moment the little old man dissolved in the clear morning. But the red speck of his lantern kept on running and leaping imprudently between the rails to meet the train.

In the distant landscape the train was noisily approaching.

The Disciple

Of black satin, bordered with ermine and thick loops of silver and ebony, Andrés Salaino's cap is the most beautiful one I have ever seen. The master bought it from a Venetian merchant and it is really worthy of a prince. So as not to offend me, he stopped when passing through the old market and picked out this grey felt cap for me. Then, wishing to celebrate the caps, he had us each model for the other.

Overcoming my resentment, I sketched a head of Salaino, the best piece of work that has come from my hand. Andrés appears with his beautiful cap and the haughty gesture with which he walks through the Florentine streets, believing himself a master of painting at the age of eighteen. In his turn, Salaino did a portrait of me with my ridiculous cap and my air of a country bumpkin recently arrived from San Sepolcro. The master seemed pleased with our efforts and he himself felt like drawing. He said, "Salaino knows how to laugh and he has not fallen into the trap." And then, turning to me, "You still believe in beauty. You will pay very dearly for it. Not one line is missing in your sketch, but there are too many of them. Bring me a canvas. I'll show you how beauty is destroyed."

With a charcoal pencil he traced the outline of a lovely figure: an angel's face or perhaps a beautiful woman's. He said to us, "Look, here is nascent beauty. These two hollows are her eyes; these imperceptible lines, the mouth. The whole face lacks contours. This is beauty." And then with a wink, "Let's finish her off." In a short while, letting some lines fall over others, creating spaces of light and shadow, he drew from memory before my marveling eyes the portrait of Gioia. The same dark eyes, the same oval face, the same imperceptible smile.

When I was most bewitched, the master interrupted his work and began to laugh strangely. "There is no more beauty here," he said. "All that remains is this infamous caricature." Uncomprehending, I kept staring at that splendid, open face. Suddenly, the master ripped the drawing in two and threw the pieces into the fire on the hearth. I was stunned. Then he did something I shall never forget nor pardon. Ordinarily so silent, he began to laugh with an odious, frenzied laughter. "Quick, go on, save your lady from the fire!" And he took me by the right hand and with it stirred the fragile ashes of the drawing. For the last time I saw Gioia's gay smile among the flames.

With my scorched hand I wept in silence, while Salaino noisily celebrated the master's crude joke.

I keep on believing in beauty. I shall not be a great painter, and in vain I have forgotten my father's tools in San Sepolcro. I shall not be a great painter, and Gioia will wed the merchant's son. But I still believe in beauty.

Greatly disturbed, I left the study and wandered about at random through the streets. Beauty was all about me, raining gold and blue over Florence. I saw it in the dark eyes of Gioia and in Salaino's arrogant bearing, topped with his beaded cap. On the riverbank I stopped to gaze down at my two inept hands.

Little by little the light fades and the Campanile casts its somber shadow across the sky. The panorama of Florence slowly darkens like a sketch on which too many lines accumulate. A bell peals signaling nightfall.

Frightened, I clutch my body and begin to run, afraid I will dissolve in the twilight. In the last clouds I think I distinguish the master's cold and disenchanted smile, which freezes my heart. I start walking again, with head cast down, along the streets which are getting darker and darker, sure that I'm going to be lost in the oblivion of mankind.

Eve

He pursued her all through the library between tables, chairs, and lecterns. She escaped, while speaking of women's rights, which had been grossly violated. Five thousand absurd years separated them. For five thousand years she had been pursued inexorably, held back, reduced to slavery. He tried to justify himself by praising his virtues rapidly and in a fragmentary fashion, uttering broken, incomplete sentences with tremulous gestures.

He searched vainly for the texts that could support his theories. The library, specializing in Spanish literature of the sixteenth and seventeenth centuries, was a great enemy arsenal bolstering the concept of honor and similar atrocious ideas.

The young man tirelessly cited J. J. Bachofen, the wise man all women should read, because he has restored to them the grandeur of their role in prehistoric times. If the savant's books were at hand, he would have confronted her with the portrait of that obscure civilization, ruled over by women when the earth had a hidden, womblike humidity in all its parts and man was trying to raise himself out of it by building lake dwellings.

But the girl was left cold by all this. That matriarchal period, unfortunately belonging to prehistoric times and scarcely provable, seemed to increase her resentment. She always got away, fleeing from one bookshelf to another; sometimes she climbed up the ladders and overwhelmed the young man with a rain of abuse. Fortunately, in his defeat something came to his aid. He suddenly remembered Heinz Wölpe. Citing this author, his voice acquired a new and powerful accent.

"In the beginning there was only one sex, evidently feminine, which reproduced itself automatically. A mediocre being began to take form sporadically, leading a precarious and sterile life faced with formidable maternity. Nonetheless, little by little it began appropriating to itself certain essential organs. The moment arrived when it became indispensable. Woman realized too late that half her elements were gone and that she needed to seek them in man, who was man by virtue of that progressive separation and that accidental return to his point of origin."

Wölpe's thesis seduced the girl. She looked tenderly at the young man. "Man is a child who has behaved badly to his mother all through history," she said, almost with tears in her eyes.

She pardoned him, pardoning all men. Her glance lost its brilliance, she lowered her eyes like a madonna. Her mouth, hard with scorn before, now became soft and sweet as a fruit. He felt mythological caresses burst from her hands and lips. Trembling, he approached Eve and Eve did not flee.

There in the library, on that complicated and negative stage, at the foot of volumes of weighty literature, the millenary episode began, just like life in the lake dwellings.

The Assassin

I do nothing but think of my assassin, that imprudent and timid young man who approached me the other day as I came from the hippodrome, at a moment when the guards would have cut him to pieces before he could manage to brush against the edge of my tunic.

I felt him throbbing with excitement near me. What he was planning to do was churning about in him like a furiously careening chariot. I saw him reach with his hand for the hidden dagger, but I helped him to contain himself by swerving slightly from my course. He looked faint, leaning against a column.

It seems to me that I have seen him other times before, a pure, unforgettable face among this bestial mob. I recall that one day a palace cook came running out after a youth who was fleeing with a knife he had robbed. I could swear that that young man is the inexpert assassin and that I shall die by the blade of that kitchen butcher knife.

The day when a band of drunken soldiers entered my house to proclaim me emperor, after dragging Rhinometos' body through the street, I realized that the die was cast. I submitted to fate, abandoning a life of opulence, softness, and vice to become a complacent executioner.

Now my turn has come. That youth, who carries my death in his hand, obsesses me with his deft persecution. Our rendezvous must be expedited, before the usurper emerges who will betray him, dealing me an ignominious tyrant's death.

Tonight I shall stroll about alone through the imperial gardens. I shall go bathed and perfumed, I shall wear a new tunic and confront the assassin, trembling behind a tree.

In the dagger's rapid thrust I shall see my gloomy soul illumined as in a lightning flash.

Small Town Affair

When he turned his head to the right side to sleep the last, brief, light, morning slumber, Don Fulgencio had to make a great effort and he gored the pillow. He opened his eyes. What up to then had been a slight suspicion now became a sharp certainty.

With a powerful movement of his neck, Don Fulgencio raised his head and the pillow flew off into the air. Before the mirror he couldn't hide his admiration for the massive curly head and splendid horns. Deep-set in his forehead, the horns were whitish at the base, jasper-green half way up, and pitch-black at the points.

The first thing Don Fulgencio thought of was to try on his hat. Frustrated, he had to push it to the back of his head, which gave him a rather foolish look.

Since having horns is not reason enough for a methodical man to interrupt his usual routine, Don Fulgencio went about getting dressed from head to foot with special care. After shining his shoes, he lightly polished his already resplendent horns.

His wife served breakfast with exquisite tact. Not one gesture of surprise did she make, nor the least allusion that might wound her noble, daredevil husband. Merely a light and fearful glance, as though not daring to rest on the sharp-pointed horns, flickered for an instant across her face.

The kiss at the door was like the bullfighting dart with its colored bow. Don Fulgencio went out on the street, snorting and pawing, ready to attack his new life. People greeted him as usual, but he noticed a torero-like feint from a youngster who yielded the sidewalk to him. An old woman who was returning from mass gave him one of those stupendous stares, as insidious and unblinking as a long snake's. When, offended, he started charging her, the owlish creature entered her house like a matador going into the shelter at the bullring. Don Fulgencio bumped into her door, which was slammed in his face, so hard that he saw stars. Far

from being just an appurtenance, his horns were intimately connected with his whole skeleton, and he felt the blow reverberate down to his feet.

Fortunately, Don Fulgencio's profession suffered no blemish or decline. His clients flocked to him enthusiastically, for his aggressiveness in attack and defense was becoming more and more apparent. From distant lands litigants came seeking the services of a lawyer with horns.

But soon the town's quiet life took on around Don Fulgencio the exhausting rhythm of a wild fiesta, filled with rows and chaos. He charged everyone, attacking right and left on the slightest pretext. To tell the truth, nobody threw his horns in his face, nobody even saw them. But everyone took advantage of his least distraction to stick a good pair of *banderillas* in him; at the very least, the most timid were satisfied in executing a flowery, burlesque, bullfighting feint before him. Some gentlemen of medieval stripe, from conceited and honorable heights, did not scorn the occasion to give him a sharp jab with the picador's goad. Sunday serenades and national fiestas were an excuse for improvising noisy, amateur, free-for-all bullfights using Don Fulgencio as the target, and wild with rage, he would charge, attacking the most daring fighters.

Dizzied by *verónicas* and other skilled movements of the bullfighter's cape, and overwhelmed by feints and punishing passes, Don Fulgencio came to the hour of truth filled with fears and dangerous defeats, converted into a ferocious beast. He and his wife were no longer invited to any fiesta or public ceremony, and she complained bitterly about the isolation in which his mean character forced her to live.

Due to jabs, prickings, and punctures from darts, Don Fulgencio enjoyed daily bleedings, and on Sundays, ostentatious hemorrhages. But all this bloodletting was internal and went toward his heart, swollen with rancor.

His thick, short, Miura-bull neck predicted the instantaneous end of his plethoric condition. Chunky and sanguine, he kept on attacking in every direction, incapable of diet or rest. One day when he was crossing the Plaza de Armas, trotting to his favorite spot in the arena, Don Fulgencio stopped and lifted his head in fear at the sound of a distant clarion. The sound came closer, entering his ears like a deafening avalanche. With blurred eyes he saw a gigantic bullring open round him; something like a Valley of Josaphat filled with his neighbors all in bullfight regalia. The congestion then plunged to his spinal column, like the matador's thrust to the withers. And Don Fulgencio keeled over, his legs in the air, without the dagger thrust.

Despite his profession, the notorious lawyer left his testament in rough draft. In it he expressed in a surprisingly suppliant tone his last wish that when he died his horns be cut off, either by saw or chisel and hammer. But his touching request was betrayed by the diligence of an officious carpenter, who made him the present of a special coffin fitted with two showy lateral additions.

The whole town, moved by the memory of his bravura, accompanied Don Fulgencio when he was dragged dead from the arena. And in spite of the sad apogee of the offerings, exequies, and condolences given the widow, the funeral services had an indefinable air of a jolly, merry masquerade.

The Song of Peronelle

From her sunny apple orchard Peronelle de Armentières sent William her first amorous rondel. She put the verses in a basket of fragrant fruit, and the message came like a spring sunbeam into the poet's dark life.

William de Machaut had turned seventy. His body, plagued

with aches and pains, was beginning to bend over toward the ground. One of his eyes was forever dimmed. Only now and then, when he heard his old verses recited by young lovers, did his heart quicken. But when he read Peronelle's song, he was rejuvenated, he took up his rebec, and that night there was no more gallant serenader in all the city.

He bit into the firm and fragrant apples, thought about the sender's youth, and his old age retreated like a shadow pursued by a ray of light. He answered her with a long and ardent letter, sprinkled with youthful poems.

Peronelle received his answer and her heart beat fast. She could think of nothing else but how she would appear one morning in festive garb before the eyes of the poet who celebrated her unknown beauty.

However, she had to wait until the festival of St. Dionysus in the fall. Accompanied by a faithful servant, she was allowed by her parents to make the pilgrimage to the sanctuary. Letters went back and forth, each time more inflammatory, bringing expectations to a peak.

At the first stopping place along the road, the master, ashamed of his years and his unseeing eye, waited for Peronelle. His heart tight with anguish, he was writing verses and a musical accompaniment to greet her with when she arrived.

Peronelle approached wrapped in the splendor of her eighteen years, incapable of perceiving the ugliness of the man who anxiously awaited her. The old servant woman couldn't get over her surprise at seeing how Master William and Peronelle passed the hours reciting rondelles and ballades, holding hands and trembling like bride and groom on the eve of their wedding.

Despite the ardor of his poems, William knew how to love Peronelle with the pure love of an old man. For her part, she looked indifferently at the young men who passed by her along the route. Together they visited the holy churches and together they took shelter at the roadside inns. The faithful servant spread her blankets between the two beds and St. Dionysus blessed the purity of this idyll when the two lovers knelt, with hands clasped together, at the foot of his altar.

But on the way back, on a splendid afternoon when about to part, Peronelle granted the poet her greatest favor. With fragrant mouth she lovingly kissed the master's withered lips. And William de Machaut wore over his heart until he died the golden hazelnut leaf which Peronelle stuck in between with her kiss.

Autrui

Monday. The systematic persecution by that unknown man continues. I think his name is Autrui. I don't know when he began to imprison me. Perhaps from the very beginning of my life without my realizing it. So much the worse.

Tuesday. Today I was calmly walking along streets and through plazas. Suddenly I noticed that my steps were taking me to unaccustomed places. The streets seemed to be laid out in a labyrinth of Autrui's design. I finally found myself in an alley with no exit.

Wednesday. My life is confined to a narrow zone in a wretched district. Useless to venture farther away. Autrui waits for me on every corner, ready to block off the great avenues from me.

Thursday. From one moment to the next I fear I shall find myself face to face and alone with the enemy. Locked in my room ready to throw myself into bed, I feel naked under Autrui's glance.

Friday. I have spent all day at home, incapable of the least activity. At night there surged around me a continuous circumvallation, a kind of ring, hardly more dangerous than a barrel hoop.

Saturday. I awoke in a hexagonal box no bigger than my body. Without daring to attack the walls, I felt that behind them new hexagonals awaited me. Doubtless, my confinement has been Autrui's work.

Sunday. Embedded in my cell, I slowly decompose. I secrete a thick, yellowish liquid of deceitful reflection. I advise no one to take me for honey—

Nobody, of course, except Autrui himself.

Sinesius of Rhodes

The oppressive pages of Paul Migne's *Patrologia griega* have buried the faint memory of Sinesius of Rhodes, who proclaimed the terrestrial empire of the angels of chance.

With his habitual exaggeration Origenes gave excessive importance within the celestial economy to the angels. For his part, pious Clement of Alexandria recognized a guardian angel hovering over us for the first time, and among the first Christians of Asia Minor an unruly affection for hierarchical proliferation was propagated.

In the obscure mass of heretical angelologists, Valentine the Gnostic and Basilides, his euphoric disciple, emerge with Luciferian brilliance. They fostered the maniacal cult of the angels. In the middle of the second century they tried to lift off the ground heavy, positivist creatures bearing lovely, scientific names like Dynamo and Sophia, to whose bestial progeny mankind owes its misfortunes.

Less ambitious than his predecessors, Sinesius of Rhodes accepted Paradise just as it was conceived by the Fathers of the Church, and contented himself with emptying it of its angels. He said that the angels live among us and that we should say all our prayers to them, as exclusive concessionaires and distributors of human possibilities. By a supreme mandate, the angels provoke, distribute, and implement the thousands and thousands of life's accidents. They make them cross and interweave with one another in an accelerated and apparently arbitrary motion. But in God's eyes they are weaving a web of complicated arabesques, far more beautiful than the night sky filled with stars. These random patterns become transformed before the eternal glance into mysterious cabalistic ciphers narrating the world's adventure story.

Sinesius' angels, like innumerable and swift shuttlers, have been weaving life's plot since the beginning of time. They fly ceaselessly to and fro, receiving and delivering decisions, ideas, experiences, and memories within an infinite, communicating brain, whose cells are born and die with men's ephemeral lives.

Tempted by the Manichean apogee, Sinesius of Rhodes had no objection to including Lucifer's hordes in his theory, and he admitted these devils as saboteurs. They complicate the warp the angels are weaving; they break the good thread of our thoughts, they alter the pure colors, they steal the silk, gold, and silver, and put coarse hemp threads in their place. Humanity offers to God's eyes its lamentable tapestry of lines sadly altered from the original design.

Sinesius spent his life recruiting laborers who would work on the side of the good angels, but he had no followers worthy of esteem. We only know that Faustus of Milevius, the Manichean patriarch, when he was old and withered and returning from that memorable African interview in which he was decisively bested by St. Augustine, stopped at Rhodes to listen to the sermons of Sinesius, who tried to win him over to his futureless cause. Faustus listened to the angelophile's petitions with senile deference, and agreed to charter a small ramshackle boat which the apostle foolhardily boarded with all his disciples, bound for a continental campaign. Nothing further was heard of them after they left the shores of Rhodes on a day when a storm was brewing.

Sinesius' heresy lacked renown and became lost on the Christian horizon without any apparent trace. It didn't even receive the honor of being officially condemned in council, despite the fact that Eutiches, the abbot of Constantinople, presented to the members of the synod an extensive refutation, which nobody read, entitled *Contra Sinesius*.

The faint memory of him has been shipwrecked on a sea of pages, Paul Migne's *Patrologia griega*.

Monologue of the Man Who Won't Give In

I possessed the orphaned girl in the candles' flickering light the very night of her father's wake. (Oh, if I could only express this in other words!)

As everything becomes known in this world, this deed reached the ears of the little old man who watches over our century behind his malicious glasses. I am referring to that ancient gentleman presiding over Mexican literature with his old-fashioned scribe's night cap, who struck me right in the street with his furious cane before the inefficient local police. I also received a corrosive rain of insults uttered in a sharp and angry voice. All this thanks to the fact that the erring patriarch—may the Devil take him—was in love with the same sweet girl who now hates me.

Woe is me! Now even the laundress hates me, despite our frank and long love affair. And the lovely confidante, whom people call my Dulcinea, refuses to listen to the complaints of her poet's grieving heart. I think even the dogs are scornful of me.

Fortunately, this infamous gossip cannot reach my beloved public. I sing for an audience composed of proper young ladies and doddering old men with positivist ideas. The atrocious rumor does not reach them; they are far removed from worldly noises. For them I am still the pale young man invoking God in imperious tercets and wiping away his tears with a lock of blond hair.

I am riddled with debts to the critics of the future. I can only pay with what I have. I inherited a sack of worn metaphors. I am one of those prodigal sons who squander their ancestors' money but cannot make a fortune with their own hands. All the things that have occurred to me were wrapped up in a depressing metaphor. And I have not been able to tell anybody the atrocious adventure of my lonely nights when God's seed began suddenly to take root in my empty soul.

There is a devil who punishes me by making me ridiculous. He dictates almost everything I write. My poor fading soul is being swept away by the avalanche of strophes.

I know very well that if I led a little more healthy and reasonable life I could be in good shape for the next century, where a new poetry is awaiting those who manage to save themselves from this disastrous nineteenth century. But I feel condemned to go on repeating myself and others.

I can already imagine my role then and the young critic who will say to me with his usual elegance, "You, dear sir, move back a little, if you don't mind. There among the representatives of our romanticism."

At the age of eighty I would go about representing former styles, with my mane of hair filled with cobwebs and my poems getting more and more hollow and ineffectual. No sir. You shall not say to me, "Move back a little, please." I am leaving right now. That is to say, I prefer to stay here in this comfortable romantic tomb, reduced to my role of a bud snipped off, a seed blown away by the icy breath of scepticism. Thanks for your good intentions.

The young ladies in rose-colored dresses will weep for me at the foot of hundred-year-old cypresses. There will always be a senile positivist to applaud my swollen rhetoric and a sardonic young man who understands my secret and sheds a hidden tear for me.

Fame, which I loved when I was eighteen, seems to me at twenty-four something like a mortuary crown rotting and stinking in the dankness of a grave.

I should truly like to do something diabolic, but nothing occurs to me. At least, I should like to find not only in my case, but all through Mexican literature, some of the odor of bitter almonds exuding from the liquor which I am ready to drink to your health, ladies and gentlemen.

Epitaph

With a well-aimed stone he cut short the abject life of Phillip Sermoyse, a bad cleric and worse friend. He shared in the spoils of two hundred shields robbed from the College of Navarre, and twice he found himself with the hangman's rope around his neck. But both times the mercy of our good King Charles came to save him in the dark dungeon.

Pray to God for him. He was born in an evil time, when hunger and plague devastated the city of Paris, when the brilliant glare of Joan of Arc's bonfire lit up terrified faces, and when the underworld argot was stuffed with English words.

By the dying light of the winter moon he saw packs of wolves come to the very pantheon of the Innocents. And he himself was like a gaunt, hungry wolf that someone had let loose in the middle of the city. He stole bread when he was hungry and seized fried fish from the very skillets of the fishvendors.

He was born in an evil time. Troops of famished children wandered the streets begging for bread. Beggars and the sick filled the naves of Our Lady to overflowing, even ascended to the presbytery and interrupted the services.

He took refuge in the church and the bordello. The old canon, his uncle, gave him the good fame of his name, and Fat Margot gave him her golden bread and repugnant body. He sang of the misfortunes of old Hëaulmière and the disdain of Catherine of Vaussels; humbly, through the mouth of his mother, he told of the glories of the Virgin Mary. In a proud tapestry the fair ladies of another time passed in a cortège through his verses, followed by the submissive and melancholy refrain. His testament favored everyone in burlesque and tragic fashion. Like a merchant in the bazaar, he displayed the gems and baubles of his soul in the public square.

Bare and scrawny as a winter turnip, he loved Paris, a soiled, impoverished city. He learned human and divine letters at Robert de Sorbon's illustrious university, where he was given a Master's degree.

But he always rolled from one misery to another. He knew the winter without fire, jail without friends, and frightful hunger on the roads of France. His companions were thieves, ruffians, deserters, and counterfeiters, all pursued or executed by the law.

He lived in an evil time. He vanished in mystery at the age of thirty. Hounded by hunger and fatigue, he fled like a dying wolf seeking the darkest corner of the forest. Pray to God for him.

The Prodigious Milligram

> ". . . moverán prodigiosos miligramos."
> Carlos Pellicer

An ant, censured because of the subtle loads she brought home and because of her frequent distractions, one day found a prodigious milligram when she wandered off the road again. Without stopping to think about the consequences of her find, the ant picked up the milligram and placed it on her back. Joyously, she ascertained that the object was just the right weight, giving a strange energy to her body, like the wings on a bird. It is true that one of the causes that bring on ants' deaths is the way they do not take into account the strength of their own forces. After delivering a grain of corn at the granary, which she has carried for a mile, the ant scarcely has strength enough left to drag her body to the cemetery.

The ant didn't realize how important her discovery was, but her pace betrayed the anxious speed of one fleeing with a treasure. A vague and wholesome feeling of having discovered something began to make her spirit swell. After deliberately and happily taking a long roundabout way, the ant joined her string of companions all returning at nightfall with the cargo solicited that day: carefully snipped off tiny bits of lettuce leaves. The road of ants formed a thin and wavering crest of diminutive greenness. It was impossible to deceive anyone: the milligram was violently out of tone in that perfect uniformity.

Once at the anthill things turned very grave. The guardians at the door and the inspectors located in all the galleries made more and more serious objections to the strange cargo. The words "milligram" and "prodigious" came here and there from the lips of some who were very knowledgeable. Until the chief inspector, seated gravely before an imposing table, dared to gather them together saying scornfully at the astonished ants: "Probably you have brought us a prodigious milligram. I congratulate you with all my heart, but my duty is to call the police." Police officers are the people least apt to solve questions of prodigies and milligrams. Faced with a case not covered in the penal code, they proceeded with aplomb to go by their ordinary laws, confiscating the milligram and taking the ant into custody too. Since the background of the accused ant was appalling, a trial was adjudged in order. The competent authorities took charge of the matter.

The habitual slowness of judiciary procedures clashed with the

ant's anxiety, and the ant's strange behavior predisposed her unfavorably even with her own lawyers. Obeying the dictates of her
convictions, which became ever firmer, the ant responded haugh-
tily to all the questions put to her. She spread the rumor that in her
case very grave injustices were being committed, announcing that
very soon her enemies would have to recognize the importance of
her find. Such wild accusations brought down upon her all sanctions available. With extravagant arrogance the ant sincerely la-
mented that she formed a part of such an imbecilic anthill. On
hearing these words, the public prosecutor asked in stentorian
tones for the death sentence.

At that moment the testimony of a celebrated alienist, who
clearly described the ant's unbalanced mental state, came to her
rescue. At night, instead of sleeping, the prisoner turned her milligram over and over, polishing it carefully, and spending many
long hours in a kind of contemplative ecstasy. During the day she
carried the milligram on her back from one side to another in the
narrow, dark jail. The ant approached the end of her life in so
great an agitation that the doctor on guard asked three times that
her cell be changed. Each time the cell was larger, but the ant's
agitation grew as the space increased. She did not pay the slightest
attention to all the curious ants who, in growing numbers, came
to contemplate her agony. She stopped eating almost completely,
refused to receive newspapermen, and kept absolute silence.

The authorities finally decided to move the maddened ant to a
sanatorium. But official decisions always suffer from delay. One
day at dawn the jailer found the cell quiet and filled with a strange
splendor. The prodigious milligram was shining on the floor, like
a diamond inflamed by its own light. Nearby, with her feet in the
air, lay the heroic ant, consumed and transparent.

The news of the ant's death and the prodigious virtue of the
milligram spread like wildfire through all the galleries. Caravans

of visitors came to the cell, which had been improvised into a brightly lit chapel. The ants dashed themselves against the ground in despair. Damaged by the vision of the milligram, their eyes shed tears in such abundance that funeral arrangements were complicated by a drainage problem. As there were not enough floral offerings, the ants plundered graves and covered the victim's body with pyramids of food.

The anthill lived through indescribable days, mixed with admiration, pride, and grief. Sumptuous exequies were organized, crowned with dances and banquets. The construction of a sanctuary for the milligram was rapidly initiated, and the ant who had been misunderstood and assassinated was honored by the erection of a mausoleum. The authorities were deposed and accused of ineptness.

Shortly afterward a committee of old ants that functioned with great difficulty managed to put an end to the prolonged series of orgiastic honors. Life returned to its normal course, thanks to innumerable executions by firing squads. The wisest of the old ants then guided the current of devout admiration that the milligram had awakened to a more and more rigid form of official religion. Guardians and priests were named. Around the sanctuary a circle of huge buildings was being built, and an extensive and rigidly hierarchical bureaucracy began to occupy them. The flourishing anthill's economic capacity was seriously compromised.

Worst of all was that disorder, dispelled from the surface, thrived anxiously underground. Apparently, the anthill lived compact and calm, dedicated to its work and cult, despite the large number of functionaries who spent their lives discharging tasks each day less appreciated. It is impossible to say which ant harbored in its mind the first gloomy thoughts—many at the same time perhaps, falling into temptation.

In any case, there were ambitious and dazzled ants who considered, blasphemously, the humble condition of the ant who had made the discovery. They foresaw the possibility that all the homage attributed to the glorious dead ant might be entrusted to them during their lives. They began to take on suspicious attitudes. Melancholy and rambling, they purposely wandered off the road and returned empty-handed to the anthill. They answered the inspectors without hiding their arrogance; frequently they would feign illness and announce that a sensational find was in the near future. Even the authorities could not dispel the idea that one of those lunatic ants might arrive with a prodigy on its weak back.

The ants mixed up in the business worked in secret, and let us say, for their own profit. If a general interrogation had been possible, the authorities would have reached the conclusion that fifty percent of the ants, instead of busying themselves with their wretched cereal grains and fragile vegetable bits, were keeping their eyes fixed on the incorruptible substance of the milligram.

One day what had to happen did happen. As if by agreement, six of the ordinary ants who seemed to be most normal, arrived at the anthill each with a strange object which they passed off as prodigious milligrams. Naturally, they did not obtain the honors they were expecting, but they were exonerated that same day from further service, and a life-time income was granted them.

It was impossible to say anything concrete about the six milligrams. The memory of former imprudence kept the authorities from handing down any legal opinions. The old ants washed their hands in council and gave to the populace great freedom of judgment. The supposed milligrams were offered for public admiration in the display windows of a modest corner, and all the ants gave out opinions according to their reliable knowledge and understanding.

This weakness on the part of the authorities, together with the critics' guilty silence, hastened the anthill's ruin. From then on any ant, exhausted by work or tempted by laziness, could limit her ambitions of glory to a lifetime pension, free of servile obligations. And the anthill began to get filled with false milligrams.

In vain some old and sensible ants recommended precautionary measures, such as the use of scales and a detailed comparison of each new milligram with the original model. Nobody heeded them. Their proposals, that were not even discussed in assembly, ended after the words of a thin, discolored ant who proclaimed her personal opinions in a loud voice. According to this irreverent creature, the famous original milligram, however prodigious it might be, did not need to set a precedent for quality. Prodigiousness should not be imposed in any case as a condition for new-found milligrams.

The little discretion remaining to the ants disappeared in a moment. From then on the authorities were incapable of reducing or assaying the quota of objects the anthill could daily receive under the title of milligrams. They were denied any right of veto whatsoever, and they couldn't even make each ant fulfill her obligations. All wanted to avoid their workers' status by looking for milligrams.

The deposit for these articles came to occupy two-thirds of the anthill, without counting private collections, some of them famous for the value of their pieces. The price of common milligrams plummeted, so that in days of greatest abundance they could be obtained in exchange for any trifle. One cannot deny that from time to time some estimable examples reached the anthill. But they suffered the fate of the worst of the worthless ones. Legions of amateurs devoted themselves to exalting the merit of milligrams of the most dubious quality, fomenting general discord in this way.

In their desperation at finding no authentic milligram, many ants brought back true obscenities and horrors. Entire galleries were closed up for reasons of health. One extravagant ant's example brought forth thousands of imitators the next day. With great effort and employing all their reserves of common sense, the old ants on the council continued calling themselves authorities and made vague gestures of governing.

The bureaucrats and members of the cult, not content with their easy lot, abandoned the temple and the offices to throw themselves into the search for milligrams, trying to increase their emoluments and honors. The police practically ceased to exist, and uprisings and revolutions were daily occurrences. Bands of professional assaulters waited near the anthill to plunder the unfortunate ants returning with a valuable milligram. Jealous collectors denounced their rivals and provoked long trials, seeking revenge for having their properties searched and expropriated. The disputes in the gallery easily degenerated into fights, and the fights into assassinations. The mortality rate reached a frightful figure. Births diminished in an alarming fashion, and children, lacking adequate attention, died by the hundreds.

The sanctuary containing the true milligram was converted into a forgotten tomb. The ants, who were busy discussing the most scandalous finds, didn't even go to visit it. Now and then some devout backward ant called the authorities' attention to its ruinous abandoned state. All it would get was a little cleaning. Half a dozen disrespectful street sweepers would give a few sweeps with their brooms, while decrepit old ants pronounced long speeches and covered the tomb with deplorably trashy offerings.

Buried in clouds of disorder, the prodigious milligram shone in oblivion. There even circulated the scandalous notion that it had been robbed by sacrilegious hands. A copy of bad quality supplanted the authentic milligram, which now belonged to the collection of the criminal ants, enriched in the milligram business. All rumors without foundation—but nobody was upset or cared, nobody carried out an investigation to put an end to them. And the old ants on the council, getting weaker and more sickly every day, crossed their arms in the face of the imminent disaster.

Winter was approaching and the threat of death stopped the delirium of the ants who had made no provision. Faced with a food crisis, the authorities decided to offer a huge lot of milligrams for sale to a neighboring community composed of well-to-do ants. All they managed was to strip themselves of a few pieces of real value in exchange for vegetables and grain. But they were made an offer of food sufficient to last them through the winter for the original milligram.

The bankrupt anthill clung to its milligram as though it were a lifesaver. After interminable conferences and discussions, when hunger had reduced the number of survivors to the benefit of the rich ants, the latter opened the door of their house to the owners of the prodigy and took on the obligation of feeding them until the end of their days, freed from all service. When the last foreign ant died, the milligram would become the property of the buyers.

Is it necessary to say what happened shortly afterward in the new anthill? The guests spread the germ of their contagious idolatry there.

Now the ants are faced with a universal crisis. Forgetting their customs, traditionally practical and utilitarian, they give themselves over everywhere to an unrestrained search for milligrams. They eat outside the anthill and only store up dazzling, unusual objects. Perhaps very soon they will disappear as a zoological species, and we will have left, enclosed in two or three ineffectual fables, only the memory of their virtues.

Cocktail Party

"I had the most marvelous time!" said Monna Lisa in her falsetto voice, and the imbeciles bowed reverently before her, a chorus of open-mouthed frogs. Her laughter dominated the palace salon like the solo jet of a silly fountain. (That night when the streams of bitterness penetrated to my bones.)

"I had the most marvelous time!" I attended the party as a representative of the spirit, and on every hand I received congratulations, handshakes, caviar canapés, and cigarettes, after having shown my credentials. (In reality, I had only gone to see Monna Lisa.) "What are you painting these days?" The monsters in brocade and precious stones were coming and going in the smoky, burbling, venomous myrtle aquarium. Blind with anger and making my phosphorus lantern shine in the shadow, I tried to attract Monna Lisa's attention toward the great profundities, but she only nibbled on superficial baits, and the elegant people there with their pompous talk devoured her with their eyes.

"I had the most marvelous time!" Finally I had to hide myself in a corner, surrounded by false disciples, my glass of hemlock in my hand. An elderly lady approached to tell me she wanted to have something of mine in her home: a surprise cake for her next banquet, a bathtub with a single spigot for both hot and cold water, or some snowy statues like those lovely ones that Michelangelo modeled in the winter at the Medici palace. In my capacity as representative of the spirit I courteously rejected all the lady's insinuations, but I assisted her in giving birth to her difficult ideas. I stayed a little longer until I had drained the dregs of my last highball and had the opportunity to bid Monna Lisa goodbye. At the threshold of the door, with her face lost in her fur coat, she sincerely confessed to me, just between us, that she'd had the most marvelous time.

Aristotle's Lay

On the grass in the meadow Aristotle's muse is dancing. The old philosopher turns his head from time to time and contemplates the youthful, pearly body for a moment. His hands let the crackling papyrus roll fall to the ground, while his blood courses fast and hot through his decrepit body. The muse dances on in the meadow, unfolding before his eyes a complicated choreography of lines and rhythms.

Aristotle thinks about the body of a girl, a slave at the market of Stagira, whom he could not buy. He remembers too that from then on no other woman has disturbed his mind. But now when his back is bent by the weight of years and his eyes are beginning to fill with shadow, the muse Harmony comes to take away his tranquility. In vain he sets cool meditations against her beauty: she always returns and begins again the light and flaming dance.

It doesn't do Aristotle any good to close the window and light up his writing with a weak oil lamp; Harmony continues to dance through his brain, disturbing the serene course of his thought, which is marbled with shadow and light like churning water.

The words he is writing lose the calm gravity of dialectic prose and break into sonorous iambic. There come back to his memory on the wings of a recondite wind the vigorous phrases of his youthful language, charged with country smells.

Aristotle abandons his work and goes out to the garden, which is open like a huge flower filled with the splendors of spring. He breathes in deeply the roses' perfume and bathes his old face in the freshness of the morning dew.

The muse Harmony dances before him, winding and unwinding her interminable frieze, her labyrinth of fleeting forms where human reason goes astray. Suddenly, with unexpected agility, Aristotle rushes after the woman, who flees as though on wings, losing herself in the forest.

The philosopher returns to his cell exhausted and ashamed. He rests his head in his hands and silently weeps for the loss of his muse. When he looks at the window again, the muse resumes her interrupted dance. All of a sudden, Aristotle decides to write a treatise that will destroy Harmony's dance, upsetting all its moods and rhythms. In humiliation, he accepts verse as an inescapable condition and begins to compose his masterpiece, the treatise *De Armonia*, which burned on Omar's bonfire.

During the time he took to compose it the muse danced for him. When he wrote the last verse, the vision vanished, and the philosopher's soul rested forever, freed from beauty's sharp jabbing needle. But one night Aristotle dreamed that he was walking about on the grass on all fours during the Grecian spring and that the muse was mounted astride him. On the following day he wrote these words at the beginning of his manuscript: my verses are sluggish and ungainly like the donkey's walk, but Harmony rides upon them.

The Condemned One

> "For several weeks newspapers from Mexico City and journals from the provinces arrived at my house containing long articles about my death."
> Enrique González Martínez, *El hombre del buho*, XVI, 147–148.

When I read the news of his death, I was inspired. Suddenly I conceived *The One Chosen by the Gods,* and I was able to sketch in the first three octaves. The poetry came surging from me spontaneously and clearly.

The next day the beginning of the poem, empty of truth, disintegrated for me. The false dead one was as alive as I, putting a check on my fortune.

From that time on I fought with unequal weapons, always at a disadvantage. But at least once I was able to confront the enemy in singular duel. The palaestra, Maria Serafina's album; the inflexible acrostic, the combat weapon. My rival faltered at the fifth verse. Some yellowed pages conserve the unfinished poem, followed by my victorious triple acrostic.

Ten years after that triumph the provincial newspapers published my death notice in piously exact terms. Ten years of fighting a retreat action from trenches ever more distant, while my adventurous rival gained his laurels. During that lapse I can mention with pride only the *Wedding Sonnet* to Maria Serafina—a brief faltering of chivalry on the altar of spite—and the lyrics to the school hymn *Progress*, daily butchered by unworried executors.

My rival ignored my true stature, and destiny saved him from all risks, because his death was the indispensable condition of *The One Chosen by the Gods*, a certain masterpiece.

Every morning the angels come to read me poems by my tenacious adversary, so that I will accept his glory. When the reading is done and before I can formulate a judgment, the memory of that unfinished acrostic in Maria Serafina's album brings an adverse opinion from my mouth. Crestfallen, the angels fly away in search of new poems.

This has been going on now for some forty years. My modest coffin has already become quite deteriorated. Humidity, wood borers, and envy are destroying it, while I review and deny the grandeur of a poet who threatens my immortality.

My Daily Bread

I'm very upset over the neglect of our friend concerning my allowance . . .

My allowance should not suffer or falter or change . . .

How can my allowance be blamed, what sin has my credit committed, that I am not paid punctually? . . .

The thousand *reales* of my allowance I'll wind up discussing with St. Peter . . .

Accordingly, I beg Your Grace to see to it that Pedro Alonso de Baena sends me a draft for 8,500 *reales*, my allowance for the months from now until the end of this year . . .

I have got Don Agustín Fiesco to write Pedro Alonso de Baena about my allowance . . .

I also implore that you point out to our friend that 600 *reales* each month do not suffice as allowance for a member of the Order of St. John . . .

It will be a great favor to me to avoid trouble with them and to ask for my June allowance in the same way . . .

There is no alternative for one on allowance . . .

For the love of God, may Your Grace try to satisfy these men and aid me with the June allowance . . .

With 500 *reales* from now until the end of December an ant couldn't get by, and it is much worse for one who is honorable . . .

Tomorrow it will be January, beginning of the year and of my allowance . . .

I entreat Your Grace to get my friend to extend my allowance from now until October . . .

I thought that our friend would change his behavior during Lent as well as his diet, but I see that he proceeds in an even meaner fashion with the allowance now than before, for he conspires against my diet, making me fast even on Sundays, which the church does not require . . .

This year's allowance in writing was skimpy, but in dispensation even more so, for there has not been any . . .

To go about with no allowance in advance is to die . . .

It is not good to weary you twice over the matter of my allowance that I have implored Your Grace about . . .

And let us settle the matter of my poor allowance so that I can dine though I never sup . . .

I beg Your Grace to do something about all this, for I no longer keep track of myself or my allowance . . .

I will perish, and my credit even more, if Your Grace does not help me like the fine person you are, making them deliver my allowance in one lump sum . . .

I should like to know if my allowance is different from other people's or if to my misfortune I am more glorious than other men . . .

Our friend is making costly experiments on my nature, doubtless ascertaining what my angelic qualities are, since he lets me fast so many days . . .

My dear Don Francisco: Your Grace, who has many windmills, knows that the miller does not eat from the millclapper's noise, but from the wheat in the hopper . . .

What does my wretched food have to do with the contribution of Don Fernando de Córdoba y Cardona? . . .

And something more that will be enough to assure the extensions they might give to my allowance . . .

I implore Your Grace to please beg him on my part to give me the allowance I am to have this year . . .

It is a subterfuge on his part not only to delay paying the allowance, but to hold it back the way he does . . . .

Don't leave me so cruelly dependent on such a miserable allowance . . .

As for my allowance, I have suffered a thousand necessities all this time . . .

Four months have gone by now without my seeing one red cent of my allowance . . .

Please order and bill to my allowance one hundred pounds of dried orange blossoms, I mean the kind that have already been distilled . . .

Concerning Your Grace's offer not to forsake me in the matter of my allowance, I kiss your hands as many times as the amount of *marvedís* they contain . . .

How reasonable it would be to send me the full amount of my allowance at once instead of in driblets . . .

I am still waiting for the guarantee of my allowance . . .

There are 800, I mean 850, *reales* left of my allowance until the end of this month . . .

I have got Don Agustín Fiesco to give me 2,550 *reales*, which is the remainder of my allowance to the end of August, which is to-day, and the month of September which starts tomorrow, so that I shall have something to live on until the end of the said month of September . . .

I beg Your Grace that there be no hitch in it, because my credit and the securing of my food supply is involved . . .

It is not much to ask that my allowance for one month be paid in advance . . .

Not much is done about the pay nor about the certainty of my allowance . . .

Will Your Grace turn his back on me and write the Fiescos to deny me even my allowance? . . .

For that it is necessary to extend the provisions of my allowance . . .

He refused to give out my allowance three days in advance . . .

I implore you please to come to my rescue, because I cannot pay anything with such a small allowance . . .

I kiss Your Grace's hands over and over for advancing my allowance . . .

I beg Your Grace to please favor me with the two months' allowance I asked for . . .

I am worse off than Your Grace left me, in such bad shape that I have had to sell an ebony writing table so as to eat these two weeks, because my disappointing allowance may delay in reaching me . . .

Thanks to Cristóbal de Heredia, there are some who will trust me for bread, which I eat with bacon slices from Rute . . .

There is no light nor even twilight of comfort: night is what I live in, and what is worse, with nothing to sup on during it . . .

I consider Your Grace an intimate friend with whom I could break bread; and would it were so, for I am only under Your Grace's table, eating your crumbs and begging now that you drop me at least a slice of bread . . .

Though I complain to God and the world, they will tell me I am Don Luis de Góngora wherever I am, and especially in Madrid, where they will see that I get a well-paid allowance . . .

I kiss Your Grace's hands for what you do to support me . . .

Because 800 *reales* are slim pickings for a man of account in this place . . .

And I find myself at winter's threshold without a stitch of clothing, my allowance advanced a month and a half so I can eat . . .

Don Luis de Góngora, Letters

Notes Full of Rancor

a Antonio Alatorre

Fleeing from the spectacle of their stifling happiness, I have plunged again into loneliness. Hemmed in between four walls, I fight in vain against that repulsive image.

I bet on the breakup of their happiness and I spy in great detail on their menage. That evening I rushed off like a third party who makes a crowd. They started their love-making before my very eyes, embracing in an intense, sly way, in a secret, lascivious, conjugal embrace.

When I bid them goodbye they could scarcely conceal their haste; they were all atremble in voluptuous expectation of being alone. The two of them pushed me out of their false paradise as though I were a guest who had done something wrong. But I always drag myself back there. And when I perceive their gesture of satiety, the first sign of weariness and sadness, I shall get to my feet with a burst of laughter. I shall shake from my shoulders the unbearable burden of their happiness.

I have been waiting many nights for this to happen. The flesh, alive and fragrant with love, becomes filled with systematic worms. But there is still a lot left to gnaw away before it can settle into dust and be blown from my heart by just any gust of wind.

I looked at her spirit in the odious ebb tide that revealed a layer of miserable detritus in the light. Nonetheless, today I can still say to her, "I know you. I know you and love you. I love the greenish depths of your soul. I know how to find a thousand dark little things there that suddenly shine in my spirit."

From her false Cleopatra bed she implores and commands. A thick warm atmosphere surrounds her. After an infinite number of days' sailing, the sleeping woman runs aground on the final sands of noonday.

Deferential and submissive, the faithful slave helps her disembark from her purple scallop shell. Carefully, he loosens her from her oyster dream. Acolyte, intoxicated on the waves of a tenuous incense, the youth assists her in the monotonous rites of her unwholesome indolence. Sometimes she awakens on the high seas and spies the young man's silhouette on the beach, broken by the shadow. She thinks she is dreaming and sinks back down under the sheets. He scarcely breathes, seated on the edge of the bed. When his beloved is deep asleep, the punctual phantom gets up and really disappears, faded and melancholy, along the deserted streets of dawn. But two or three hours later he is back on the job.

The youth vanishes sadly in the deserted streets, but I am here, stricken with insomnia, like a toad deep down in a well. I strike my forehead against the wall of loneliness and I distinguish far away the shapeless indolent pair. She navigates horizontally through a thick narcotic dream, while he is rowing toward the shore, watchful, silent, tenderly cautious, like one who bears a treasure in a leaky boat.

Here I am, fallen in the night, like an anchor among the sea rocks without a ship to sustain me. Over me the bitter sea piles up its corrosive lime, its green salt sponges, its tough branches of malignant vegetation.

Sluggishly, the two delay and put off the predicted finish. The demon of passivity has seized them, and I am shipwrecked in anguish. Many nights have passed and in the room's shut-up, intimate, heavy atmosphere, one cannot detect lust's pungent odor. There is only the lingering sugary emanation of anise and a rancid smell of black olives.

The young man languishes in his corner until he gets another order. She navigates in her gondola with a halo of anesthesia. She complains, complains interminably. The young doctor at the head of her bed bends over solicitously and listens to her heart. She smiles very sweetly, like a dying heroine in the third act. Her hand falls lifelessly into the hands of the erotic Galen. Then she recovers, lights the little brazier of aromatic fumes, orders the wardrobe, crammed with clothes and shoes, to be opened, and pondering, chooses her daily garments one by one.

In the meantime, I who am shipwrecked, make desperate signals from my rock. I whirl in the spiral of insomnia. I cry out to the darkness. Slow as a diver I go through the interminable night. And they put off the decisive act, the predicted finish.

From afar my voice accompanies them. Repeating the litanies of a useless love, I am always worn out and exhausted, my mouth full of blind and rancorous words, by each pale dawn.

Nabonides

Nabonides' original proposal, according to Professor Rabsolom, was simply to restore the archeological treasures of Babylonia. Sadly he had looked at the worn stones of the sanctuary, the stele of the heroes, and the cylindrical stamps that left an illegible imprint on the imperial documents. He undertook his restoration methodically and not without a certain parsimony. Of course, he was concerned about the quality of the material, choosing stones with the finest and closest grain.

When it occurred to him to copy the eight hundred thousand tablets in the Babylonian library again, he had to establish schools and workshops for scribes, engravers, and potters. He drew away a good many employees and functionaries from their administrative posts, challenging the criticisms of the military chiefs, who were asking for soldiers and not scribes to prop up the crumbling empire, which had been built with great labor by their heroic ancestors before the envious assault of the neighboring cities. But Nabonides, who could look across the centuries, understood that history was what mattered. He gave himself valiantly to his task, while the ground gave way beneath his feet.

The gravest thing was that once all the restorations were finished Nabonides could not stop his labors as a historian. Turning his back definitively on events, he devoted himself solely to relat-

ing them on stone or clay. This clay, which he invented from a base of marl and asphalt, has proved even more indestructible than stone. (Professor Rabsolom is the one who has established the formula for ceramic paste. In 1913 he found a series of puzzling pieces, each a sort of cylinder or little column covered with that mysterious substance. Guessing that writing was hidden under them, Rabsolom realized that the asphalt paste could not be lifted without destroying the characters. Then he thought up the following procedure: he chiselled out the inner stone, then by means of a disincrustant that attacks the residue deposited in the grooves of the writing, he obtained hollow cylinders. By means of successive sectional emptying, he succeeded in making gypsum cylinders which presented the original writing intact. Professor Rabsolom shrewdly maintained that Nabonides had proceeded in this incomprehensible way, foreseeing an enemy invasion with the usual accompaniment of iconoclastic fury. Fortunately, he didn't have time to hide all his works this way.)[1]

As the multitude of workers was insufficient and history was happening rapidly, Nabonides also became a linguist and grammarian. He tried to simplify the alphabet by creating a species of shorthand. Indeed, he complicated the writing, plaguing it with abbreviations, omissions, and initials that offer a whole new series of difficulties for Professor Rabsolom. But in this way Nabonides managed to come up to his own era with enthusiastic minuteness. He succeeded in writing the history of his history and hinting at the key to his abbreviations, but with such a zeal for synthesis that this story would be as long as the *Epic of Gilgamesh* if it were compared with this last concise work of Nabonides.

He also had a history of his hypothetical military accomplishments written up—Rabsolom says he wrote it himself—he who

---

[1] Those wishing to delve deeply into this matter can profitably read the extensive monograph by Adolph von Pinches, *Nabonidzylinder*, Jena, 1912.

abandoned his sumptuous sword in the body of the first enemy warrior. Really, this history was just one more pretext for sculpting tablets, stelae, and cylinders.

But the Persian adversaries brought about from afar the dreamer's downfall. One day an urgent message from Croesus, with whom Nabonides had made an alliance, arrived at Babylonia. The historian king ordered the message and name of the messenger, the date and conditions of the pact engraved on a cylinder. But he did not come at Croesus' call. Shortly afterward the Persians fell upon the city in a surprise attack, scattering the hard-working army of scribes. The discontented Babylonian warriors scarcely put up a fight, and the empire fell, never to rise again from its ruins.

Two obscure versions about the death of history's faithful servant have come down to us. One of them has him sacrificed in the hands of a usurper during the tragic Persian invasion. The other tells us that he was made prisoner and taken to a remote island, where he died of sadness, reviewing in his memory the repertoire of Babylonian grandeur. This last version is the one most in keeping with Nabonides' peaceful nature.

You and I

Adam lived happily inside Eve in an intimate paradise, held like a seed in the sweet substance of the fruit, efficient as a gland with its internal secretions, a slumbering chrysalis in his silky cocoon, the wings of his spirit tightly folded.

Like all happy creatures, Adam hated his glory and began to search everywhere for the way out. He swam against the current in the dense waters of maternity and opened up a way by bumping with his head in the mole's tunnel to cut the soft cord of his primitive alliance.

But Adam and Eve could not live apart. Little by little they thought up a ceremonial filled with prenatal nostalgia, an intimate, obscene rite that had to commence with Adam's conscious humiliation. Kneeling as if before a goddess, he beseeched her and deposited all kinds of offerings. Then, with a voice ever more urgent and threatening, he made a formal allegation favoring the myth of eternal return. After making him beg a great deal, Eve had him get up from the ground, scattered the ashes from his hair, took off his penitent's clothing and clasped him to her breast. That was ecstasy. But the act of imitative magic produced very bad results with regard to the propagation of the species. Before the irresponsible multiplication of Adams and Eves which brought as a consequence universal grief on earth, the two of them were called to account. (With its mute clamor, Abel's blood was still fresh on the ground.)

Before the supreme tribunal, Eve limited herself half-cynically and half-modestly to making a more or less veiled exposition of her natural charms, while she recited the catalogue of wifely virtues. Her lack of feeling and lapses of memory were admirably concealed by an extensive repertory of little laughs, shows of affection, and false prudery. Finally, she gave a splendid pantomime of painful childbirth.

Adam, very formal, delivered an extensive résumé of universal history, conveniently expurgated of suffering, killings, and fraud. He spoke of the alphabet and the invention of the wheel, the odyssey of knowledge, the progress of agriculture and feminine suffrage, the religious wars and Provençal lyric poetry—

Inexplicably, he gave you and me as an example. He defined us as an ideal couple and he made me the slave of your eyes. But suddenly, only yesterday, he was the cause of that shining look, which, coming from you, separates us forever.

The Lighthouse

What Genaro is doing is horrible. He uses unexpected weapons. Our situation is becoming disgusting.

Yesterday at the table he told us a story about a cuckold. In reality it was amusing, but even if Amelia and I had been able to laugh, Genaro spoiled it with his hearty false guffaws. He said, "Is there anything funnier?" And he passed his hand across his forehead, clenching his fingers, as though searching for something. Then he laughed again. "What must it feel like to wear horns?" He didn't seem to notice our confusion at all.

Amelia was desperate. I felt like insulting Genaro, shouting the whole truth at him, rushing out and never coming back. But as always something kept me from doing it. Amelia perhaps was overwhelmed by the intolerable situation.

For some time now Genaro's behavior had surprised us. He was getting more and more foolish all the time. He accepted incredible explanations and gave us a time and place for the rashest meetings. Ten times he played the comedy of the journey but he always returned on the scheduled day. We abstained uselessly during his absence. On his return, he would bring us little presents and squeeze us tightly in an immoral fashion, practically kissing our necks, holding us excessively long against his chest. Amelia reached the point of fainting with repugnance at such embraces.

In the beginning we did things fearfully, thinking we were running a great risk. The impression that Genaro was going to discover us at any moment tinged our love with fear and shame. The thing was clean and clear in this sense. Drama really floated over us, lending dignity to guilt. Genaro has spoilt it all. Now we are wrapped in something turbid, dense, and heavy. We make love without desire, surfeited, like spouses. Little by little we have acquired the insipid custom of tolerating Genaro. His presence is insufferable because he does not hinder us; rather he facilitates the routine and provokes the weariness.

At times the messenger who brings our provisions says that they are going to close down this lighthouse. Amelia and I are secretly overjoyed. Genaro is visibly upset. "Where shall we go?" he says to us. "We're so happy here!" He sighs. Then, seeking my eyes, "You'll come with us wherever we go." And with a melancholy face he gazes at the sea.

In Memoriam

The deluxe copy, in large quarto on fine Holland paper with embossed leather binding and a faint odor of recently inked print, fell like a heavy mortuary slab on the breast of the Baroness Büssenhausen.

Through her tears this noble widowed lady read the two-page dedication, composed in reverent Germanic uncial letters. Following a piece of friendly advice, she ignored the fifty chapters of the *Comparative History of Sexual Relations,* her deceased husband's work of imperishable glory, and placed that explosive volume in an Italian book jacket.

Among scientific books published on this theme, Baron Büssenhausen's work stands out in an almost sensational fashion and finds enthusiastic readers in a public whose diversity moves even the most austere scholars to envy. (The abridged translation in English has been a sensational best seller.)

For the leaders of historical materialism this book is nothing but a bitter refutation of Engels; for theologians, the insistence of a Lutheran who sketches on the sands of satiety circles of a hell too well-defined. The psychoanalysts happily plunge into a sea of two thousand pages of the pretended subconscious. They bring to the surface infamous data: perverted Büssenhausen translates in his impersonal language the history of a soul tormented by the most depraved passions. There are all his ravings, his libidinous dreams, and secret guilts, always attributed to unexpected primitive communities, in the course of an arduous and triumphant process of sublimation.

The reduced group of anthropologists who are specialists deny Büssenhausen the name of colleague, but the literary critics grant him his greatest fortune. They all agree that his book falls within the novelistic genre and they are not niggardly in comparing it with the illustrious work of Marcel Proust and James Joyce. According to these critics, the Baron gave himself up to unfruitful research in the hours wasted in his wife's bedroom. Hundreds of stagnant pages narrate the comings and goings of a soul, pure and weak, given to doubts, from the ardent conjugal Venusberg to the gelid cave of the bookish cenobite.

Be that as it may, the most faithful friends have stretched around the Büssenhausen castle, until calmness sets in, an affectionate protective net that intercepts messages from the outside. In the deserted seignorial rooms the baroness sacrifices charms not yet faded, despite her autumn years. (She is the daughter of a celebrated entomologist, now deceased, and of a poetess, still living.)

Any reader with average gifts can extract from the book more than one unnerving conclusion. For example, that marriage originated in remote times as a punishment imposed on couples who violated the taboo of endogamy. Cooped up at home, the guilty ones suffered from the inclemencies of absolute intimacy, while their fellows outside gave themselves up to the irresponsible delights of the freest love.

Displaying a keen wisdom, Büssenhausen defines matrimony as a common characteristic of Babylonian cruelty. His imagination reaches enviable heights when he describes for us the primitive assembly of Samarra, happy in pre-Hamurabi times. The flock lived carefree and gay, sharing the generous spoils of hunt and harvest, dragging about their bunch of communal offspring. But those who succumbed to the premature or illegal anxiety for possession were justly condemned to the atrocious satiety of the desired dish.

To derive modern psychological conclusions from all this is a task which the baron realizes, in a manner of speaking, with one hand tied behind his back. Man belongs to an animal species filled with ascetic pretensions. Matrimony, which at first was a formidable punishment, soon became a passionate exercise for neurotics, an incredible pastime for masochists. Nor does the baron stop here. He adds that civilization has done very well in tightening conjugal bonds. He congratulates all religions which converted matrimony into a spiritual discipline. Exposed to a continuous contact, two souls have the possibility of perfecting each other to the highest degree of polish or of reducing each other to dust.

"Considered scientifically, matrimony is a prehistoric mill in which two rotating stones grind each other interminably to death." These are the author's very words. He failed to add that the baroness offered in opposition to his porous and calcareous, tepid soul of a believer a kind of quartz of Valkyrie-like consistency. (Now in the solitude of her bed, the widow draws dauntless radial arrises around the impalpable memory of the pulverized baron.)

One could easily heap scorn on Büssenhausen's book if it contained only the personal scruples and repressions of an old-fashioned husband, who overwhelms us with his doubts about our salvation, without taking into account other souls, ready to succumb at our side, victims of boredom, hypocrisy, petty hatreds, and pernicious melancholy. What makes it all very serious is that the baron supports each of his digressions with a mass of data. On the most preposterous page, when we see him falling into an abyss of fantasy, suddenly he emerges with an irrefutable piece of proof in his shipwrecked hands. When he speaks of hospitable prostitution, if Malinowski fails him in the Marquesas Islands, there is Alf Theodorsen in his congealed Lapp village to help him out with an example. There can be no doubt about it. If the baron makes a mistake, we must confess that science, curiously enough, agrees to be in error with him. Besides the creative, overflowing imagination of a Lévy-Brühl, he has the perspicacity of a Frazer, the preciseness of a William Eilers, and, now and again, the supreme dryness of a Franz Boas.

Nonetheless, the baron's scientific rigor frequently falters and gives way to gelatinous pages. More than one passage is cumbersome and difficult going, and the volume acquires a visceral weight when Venus' false dove flutters with the wings of a bat, or when we listen to the noise of Pyramus and Thisbe gnawing, one on each side, through a thick wall of jam. But it seems only fair to pardon the slips of a man who spent thirty years in the mill with an abrasive wife, separated from him by many degrees on the scale of human hardness.

Paying no heed to the scandalized, gleeful outcries of those who judge the baron's work a new, disguised, pornographic résumé of universal history, we join the reduced group of select spirits who see in the *Comparative History of Sexual Relations* an extensive domestic epic, consecrated to a woman of Trojan temper. The perfect wife in whose honor thousands and thousands of subversive thoughts surrendered, fenced in a two-page dedication, composed in reverent Germanic uncials: the Baroness Gunhild de Büssenhausen, née Countess of Magneburg-Hohenheim.

Balthasar Gérard, 1555–1582

To go kill the Prince of Orange. To go kill him and then collect the twenty-five thousand escudos that Phillip II offered for his head. To go alone on foot, without resources, without a pistol or knife, the kind of assassin who asks his victim for the money needed to buy the weapon for the crime—this was what a young carpenter from Dôle, Balthasar Gérard, did.

He managed to make his way through the Low Countries to his victim after grievous persecution. Famished and dead tired, he suffered innumerable delays among the Spanish and Flemish armies. He endured three years of doubts, detours, and retreats, worrying all the while that Gaspar Añastro would get there ahead of him.

The Portuguese Gaspar Añastro; a cloth merchant, was not without imagination, especially with a bait of twenty-five thousand escudos waved before him. A cautious fellow, he carefully laid his plans and chose the date for the crime. But at the last minute he decided to place an intermediary between his brain and the weapon; Juan Jáuregui would wield it for him.

Juan Jáuregui, a young twenty-year-old chap, was timid by nature. But Añastro managed to instil courage in him to the point of heroism, by using a system of subtle coercions whose secret escapes us. Perhaps he overwhelmed him with heroic readings, perhaps he provided him with talismans, perhaps he led him methodically toward the annihilation of conscience.

All we know with certainty is that on the day indicated by his patron (March 18, 1582), and during the festival celebrated in Antwerp to honor the Duke of Anjou on his birthday, Jáuregui waylaid the royal retinue and shot point blank at William of Orange. But the stupid fool had overloaded the barrel of his pistol. The weapon exploded in his hand like a grenade, and a metal splinter pierced the Prince's cheek. Jáuregui fell to the ground among the retinue, stabbed by violent sword thrusts.

For seventeen days Gaspar Añastro waited in vain for the death of the Prince. Clever surgeons managed to stop the hemorrhage by plugging up the destroyed artery night and day with their fingers. William finally pulled through, and the Portuguese, who carried in his pocket Jáuregui's will in his favor, swallowed the bitterest pill of his life. He cursed his imprudence in trusting such a clumsy young man.

Shortly afterwards fortune smiled on Balthasar Gérard, who received the tragic news from afar. The survival of the Prince, whose life seemed reserved for him, gave him new energy to continue his plans, which until then had been vague and uncertain.

In May he managed to present himself before the Prince as an emissary of the army, but he did not even have a pin to his name. With difficulty he was able to repress his desperate feelings as long as the interview lasted. In vain he mentally placed his thin hands around the Belgian's thick neck. Nevertheless, he succeeded in obtaining a new commission. William designated him to return to battle to a besieged city on the French frontier. But Balthasar could not resign himself to another withdrawal.

Depressed and suspicious, he wandered about for two months in the surroundings of the palace of Delft. He lived in the greatest misery, almost begging, trying to ingratiate himself with lackeys and cooks. But his strange and miserable aspect inspired mistrust in all.

One day the Prince saw him from one of the windows of the palace and sent a servant to take him to task for his negligence. Balthasar answered that he had no clothes for the voyage and that his shoes were practically worn out. Touched, William sent him twelve crowns.

Balthasar was delighted and went running in search of a pair of magnificent pistols under the pretext that the roads were unsafe for a messenger like himself. He loaded them carefully and returned to the palace. Saying that he needed a passport, he arrived at the Prince's rooms and uttered his request in a hollow, disturbed voice. He was told to wait a little in the patio. While waiting, he made a rapid examination of the building, planning his flight.

After a little while, when William of Orange appeared at the top of a stairway, dismissing a person who was kneeling, Balthasar briskly emerged from his hiding place and shot with excellent aim. The Prince managed to murmur a few words and collapsed on the rug dying.

In the confusion Balthasar fled to the palace stables and corrals, but he was unable to jump over a garden wall in his weakened state. There he was seized by two cooks. Taken to the porter's lodge, he maintained a grave and dignified composure. All they found on him were some pious pictures and a pair of inflated bladders with which he hoped—poor swimmer that he was—to cross the rivers and canals he might find in his path.

Naturally, nobody thought about the long delay of a trial. The mob clamored for the regicide's death. But they had to wait three days because of the Prince's funeral services.

Balthasar Gérard was hanged in the public square of Delft before an angry sea of faces whom he looked at scornfully from the reef of the scaffold. He smiled at the clumsiness of the carpenter who let his hammer go flying through the air. A woman, touched by the spectacle, was on the point of being lynched by the excited mob.

Balthasar said his prayers in a clear, distinct voice, convinced of his heroic role. He climbed the fatal ladder without help.

Phillip II paid punctually the twenty-five thousand escudos recompense to the assassin's family.

Baby H.P.

Lady of the house: convert your children's vitality into motor power. We now have on sale the marvelous Baby H.P. which has revolutionized household economy.

Baby H.P. is made of a very light resistant metal that adapts itself perfectly to the infant's delicate body by means of comfortable belts, bracelets, rings, and brooches. The ramifications of this supplementary skeleton catch each one of the child's movements, converting them into a Leyden bottle that can be placed on the back or the chest, depending on necessity. A needle pointer indicates when the bottle is full. Then, Madam, you can unhook it and plug it into a special outlet, so that it will discharge automatically. This deposit can be placed in any corner of the house and represents a precious store of electricity ready at any moment for light and heating, as well as for any of the innumerable gadgets that invade our homes nowadays.

From now on you will feel differently about the exhausting activities of your children. And you will not even lose patience at a convulsive tantrum, when you remember that it is a generous source of energy. The kicking of a nursing baby during the twenty-four hours of the day is now transformed, thanks to Baby H.P., into some useful seconds of electric blending or into fifteen minutes of radio music.

Large families can satisfy all their electrical demands by installing a Baby H.P. on each of their offspring, and even realize a small and lucrative business by transmitting a little of the extra energy to their neighbors. Big apartment buildings can satisfactorily supply electricity when there are failures in the public service by hooking up all the family deposits together.

Baby H.P. causes no physical upset or psychic disturbance in children, because it doesn't hamper or disturb their movements. On the contrary, some doctors are of the opinion that it contributes to the harmonious development of their bodies. As for their spirits, it can awaken children's individual ambition, by giving them rewards when they exceed their usual record. With this end in mind, candies and sweets are recommended, because they repay their cost many times over. The more calories added to the child's diet, the more kilowatts are stored up in the electric computer.

Children should keep their lucrative H.P. on night and day. It is important for them always to wear it to school, so the precious recess period won't be wasted, and they will return home with the accumulator overflowing with energy.

Rumors that some children die electrocuted by the current they themselves generate are completely irresponsible. The same must be said of the superstitious fear that youngsters provided with a Baby H.P. attract lightning bolts and sparks. No accident of this nature can occur, especially if the directions in the explanatory pamphlets which are given out with each apparatus are followed to the letter.

Baby H.P. is available in good stores in different sizes, models, and prices. It is a modern, durable, trustworthy apparatus, and you can hook up extensions to all its parts. It carries the factory guarantee of J. P. Mansfield & Sons of Atlanta, Illinois.

Announcement

Wherever the presence of women is difficult, onerous, or prejudicial, whether in the bachelor's bedroom or in the concentration camp, the use of Plastisex© is highly recommended. The army and navy, as well as some directors of penal and teaching establishments, provide their inmates with the services of these attractive, hygienic creatures.

We now address you, whether or not you are fortunate in love.

We will furnish you with the woman you have dreamed about all your life: she is manipulated by automatic controls and is made of synthetic materials that reproduce at will the most superficial or subtle characteristics of feminine beauty. Tall and slim, short and plump, fair or dark, redhead or platinum blonde—all are on the market. We place at your disposition an army of plastic artists, expert in sculpture and design, painting and drawing; artisans clever in molding and plaster casting; technicians in cybernetics and electronics, who can unwind a mummy of the eighteenth dynasty for you, or take out of her bath the most sparkling movie star, still splashed with water and her morning bath salts.

We have all ready to be sent out famous beauties of the past and present, but we will attend to any request and we build special models. If Madame Recamier's charms are not enough to make you forget the woman who jilted you, send us photographs, documents, measurements, clothing, and enthusiastic descriptions. She will come out exactly as ordered by means of a control board no more difficult to handle than the knobs of a television set.

If you wish and have sufficient resources, she can have eyes of emerald, turquoise, or real jet, lips of coral or ruby, teeth of pearls, and so forth. Our ladies cannot be deformed or wrinkled in any way, they conserve their smoothness of skin and round fullness of figure, they say "yes" in all living and dead languages, they sing and move to the beat of fashionable rhythms. Their faces are made up in the manner of the original models, but all kinds of variations are possible, depending on one's taste, by using the appropriate cosmetics.

The mouth, nostrils, inner part of the eyelids, and other mucous regions are made of very soft sponge, saturated with hot, nutritive substances of a variable viscosity and with different vitamin and aphrodisiac contents extracted from sea weeds and medicinal plants. "There is milk and honey under your tongue . . ." says the *Song of Songs*. You can emulate Solomon's pleasures; make a mixture of goat's milk and honey, fill the cranial deposit of your Plastisex© with it, season with Port or Benedictine: you will feel the rivers of paradise flowing into your mouth in a long nourishing kiss. (Up to now we have reserved under patent the right to adapt the mammary glands as round flasks of liquor.)

Our Venuses are guaranteed to give perfect service for ten years —the average time any wife lasts—except in cases where they are subjected to abnormal sadistic practices. Like all flesh-and-blood women, their weight is rigorously specific and ninety percent of it corresponds to the water that circulates through the very fine bubbles of their spongy bodies, heated by a venous electric system. In this way one gets the perfect illusion of muscles rippling under the skin and the hydrostatic balance of masses of flesh in movement. When the thermostat reaches a degree of feverish temperature, a slightly saline discharge comes to the skin's surface. The water not only fulfills physical functions of variable plasticity, but also clearly physiological and hygienic ones: making it flow out swiftly from the inside assures the rapid and complete cleaning process of the Plastisex©.

A magnesium framework, unbreakable even in the most passionate embraces and finely designed from the human skeleton, assures a naturalness in all the Plastisex©'s movements and positions. With a bit of practice she can dance, fight, do gymnastic exercises or acrobatics, and produce in her body more or less energetic reactions of welcome or rejection. (Though submissive, the Plastisex© is extremely vigorous, since she is equipped with an electric motor of one-half horse power.)

With regard to hair, we have managed to produce an acetate fibre that has all of real hair's characteristics and that is superior to it in beauty, texture, and elasticity. Are you fond of olfactory pleasures? Then tune in your scale of odors. From the tenuous armpit aroma made from a base of sandalwood and musk to the strongest emanations of the sunburned, sports-minded woman: pure butyric acid or the most highly refined products of modern perfumery. Get intoxicated to your fill.

The olfactory and gustatory scale naturally extends to the breath; yes, indeed, for our Venuses breathe regularly or heavily. A regulator assures the rising curve of their desires, from sighs to moans, by means of the controllable rhythm of their respiratory system. The heart beats slow or fast automatically in rhythm with their breathing—

As far as accessories go, the Plastisex© rivals in her dress and adornment the most distinguished ladies. Nude, she is simply un-excelled: pubescent or not, in the flower of youth, or with all autumn's ripe opulence, according to the particular coloring of each race or mixture of races.

For jealous lovers we have improved on the ancient ideal of the chastity belt: a box for the whole body which converts each woman into a fortress of impregnable steel. As for virginity, each Plastisex© is provided with a device which only you can violate, the plastic hymen, which is a true stamp of guarantee. It is so faith-ful to the original, that when destroyed, it contracts on itself and produces coraline excrescences called myrtiform caruncles.

Following the inflexible line of commercial ethics that we have set down, we wish to denounce the more or less undercover rumors that some neurotic clients have circulated about our Venuses. It is said that we have created so perfect a woman, that some models, ardently loved by solitary men, have become pregnant, and that others suffer certain periodic disturbances. Nothing could be more false. Though our research department works at full capacity and with a tripled budget, we cannot yet boast of having so freed flesh-and-blood women from such grave physical servitude. Unfor-tunately, it is not so easy to disprove a news item published by an irresponsible journal asserting that an inexpert young man died by asphyxiation in the arms of a plastic woman. Without denying the possibility of such an accident, we affirm that it could only happen because of unpardonable carelessness.

Our industry's moral aspect has been insufficiently interpreted up to now. Along with the sociologists who praise us for having struck a hard blow at prostitution (in Marseille there is a house which can no longer be called of ill repute, because it functions exclusively with Plastisex©), there are others who accuse us of encouraging maniacs affected with infantilism. Such fearful people deliberately forget that the qualities of our invention, far from being limited to physical pleasure, assure dearly beloved intellectual and aesthetic pleasures to each one of their fortunate users.

Religious sects have reacted in very diverse ways to the problem, as was to be expected. The most conservative continue implacably supporting the habit of abstinence, and, at the most, limit themselves to qualifying as a pardonable sin one committed on an inanimate object (!). But one dissident Mormon sect has already celebrated numerous marriages between progressive human gentlemen and enchanting synthetic dolls. Though we reserve our opinion about these unions, illicit to the general public, we are very gratified to announce that up to now they have all been happy in most respects. Only in isolated cases has some husband asked for changes or perfecting of details in his wife, without one substitution equivalent to divorce being registered. Also frequent are cases of formerly married clients who ask us for faithful copies of their wives (generally with some retouches), so as to use them without betrayal during grave or passing illnesses, and during prolonged and involuntary absences, including abandonment and death.

As an object of pleasure, Plastisex© should be employed prudently and in moderation, just as popular wisdom counsels in regard to our traditional mate. Normally used, her conjugal obligations assure man's health and well-being, whatever his age or constitution. Regarding investment and maintenance expenses, Plastisex© pays for herself. She consumes as much electricity as a refrigerator, she can be plugged into any household outlet, and equipped with her most valuable attachments, she soon turns out to be much more economical than an ordinary, run-of-the-mill wife. She is inert or active, talkative or silent as you wish, and you can keep her in the closet.

Far from representing a threat to society, the Plastisex© Venus becomes a powerful ally in the fight to restore human values. Instead of diminishing women, she exalts and dignifies them, snatching from them their role as instruments of pleasure, or sexophore, to use a classical term. Instead of a depressing, costly or unhealthy piece of merchandise, our women will be converted into beings capable of developing their creative possibilities to a high degree of perfection.

When the use of Plastisex© becomes popularized we will witness the birth of feminine genius, so long awaited. Women, freed then from their traditionally erotic obligations, will establish forever in their transitory beauty the pure reign of the spirit.

On Ballistics

> "Ne saxa ex catapultis latericium discuterent."
> Caesar, *De bello civili*, 2.

> "Catapultae turribus impositae et quae spicula mitterent, et quae saxa."
> Appianus, *Ibericae*.

"Those vague·scars you see there among the tilled fields are the remains of Nobilior's camp. Beyond them rise up the military fortresses of Castillejo, Renieblas, and Peña Redonda. Of the remote city there only remains a hill steeped in violence—"

"Please! Don't forget that I've come from Minnesota. Stop this fine talk and tell me what, how, and at what distance the ballistae were shot."

"You ask the impossible."

"But you are recognized as a universal authority on ancient war machines. Professor Burns at Minnesota did not hesitate to give me your name and address as a sure guide."

"Give your professor, whom I esteem very much from our correspondence, my thanks and my sincere condolences regarding his optimism. By the way, what has happened to his experiment on Roman ballistics?"

"A complete failure. Before a large crowd Professor Burns promised to shoot it over the Minnesota stadium fence, and the home run failed. It is the fifth time that a catapult has not worked for him and he's quite dejected. He's waiting for me to bring back some data that will put him on the right track, but you—"

"Tell him not to get discouraged. The ill-fated Ottokar von Soden spent the best years of his life baffled by a *ctesibia machina* that functioned by compressed air. And Gatteloni, who knew more than Professor Burns and probably more than I, failed in 1915 with a stupendous machine based on the descriptions of Ammiano Marcelinus. Some four centuries earlier, another Florentine mechanic named Leonardo da Vinci wasted his time constructing enormous crossbows, according to the misleading indications of the celebrated amateur Marcus Vitruvius Polonius."

"I'm surprised and offended at the language that you, such a devotee of the machine, employ in referring to Vitruvius, one of the brightest geniuses of our science."

"I don't know what you and your professor think of this dangerous man. I think Vitruvius is a simple amateur. Please read his *Libri decem* very carefully, and at every turn you will realize that he is talking about things he doesn't understand. But he does transmit to us, without order or unity, to be sure, very valuable

Greek texts ranging from Aeneus the Tactical to Heron of Alexandria."

"This is the first time I've heard such disrespect. On whom then can one pin one's hopes? Perhaps Sextus Julius Frontinus?"

"Read his *Stratagematon* with the greatest caution. At first sight one has the impression of having hit upon a real find. But one is soon disenchanted by his errors and tedious descriptions. Frontinus knew a lot about aqueducts, sewers, and drains, but when it comes to ballistics he is incapable of calculating a simple parabola."

"Please don't forget that on my return I must prepare a professional thesis of two hundred pages on Roman ballistics and give some lectures. I do not want to be shamed as my professor was at the Minnesota stadium. Please cite for me some ancient authorities on the subject. Professor Burns, with his stories full of repetitions and tangents, has filled my mind with confusion."

"Allow me from here to congratulate Professor Burns on his great loyalty. I see that he has done nothing but transmit to you a chaotic vision of ancient ballistics that men like Marcelinus, Arrianus, Diodorus, Josephus, Polibius, Vegecius, and Procopius have given us. I'm going to speak clearly. We do not possess even one contemporary sketch, not one single concrete datum. The pseudo-ballistae of Justus Lipsius and Andrea Palladius are pure paper inventions absolutely lacking in reality."

"Then what shall I do? I beg of you to think of my thesis and its two hundred pages, and the two thousand words of each lecture at Minnesota."

"I'm going to tell you an anecdote that will help you to understand."

"Go ahead."

"It refers to the taking of Segida. Of course, you recall that this city was occupied by the consul Nobilior in 153."

"Before Christ?"

"It seems to me, or rather, it seemed to me, unnecessary to make such observations to you—"

"Pardon me."

"All right. Nobilior took Segida in 153. What you surely don't know is that the loss of the city, a key point on the march on Numancia, was due to a ballista."

"What a relief! An efficient ballista."

"Only in a figurative sense. But let me go on."

"Finish your anecdote. I'm sure I shall return to Minnesota without being able to say anything positive."

"The consul Nobilior, who was a spectacular man, tried to open the attack with a great catapult shot—"

"Excuse me, but we are speaking of ballista—"

"You and your famous Minnesota professor, can you tell me perhaps what the difference is between a ballista and a catapult and between a fundibula, doribula, and palintona? Concerning ancient machines, Don José Almirante has already said that the orthography is not fixed and the explanation is not satisfactory. Here are all these names for the same apparatus: petrobola, litobola, pedrera or petraria, and you can also call any machine that functions by tension, torsion, or counterweight onagro, monancona, polibola, acrobalista, quirobalista, toxobalista, and neurobalista. As all these apparatuses have been generally locomotive since the fourth century B.C., they all should justly be called carrobalistas."

"—"

"It's certainly true that the secret that made these war iguanodons work has been lost. Nobody knows how the wood was tempered, how the ropes made of esparto, horsehair, or tripe were treated, how the system of counterweight functioned."

"Continue your anecdote before I decide to change the subject of my professional thesis and expel the imaginary listeners from my lecture hall."

"Nobilior, who was a spectacular man, tried to open the attack with a great ballista shot—"

"I see that you have your anecdotes perfectly memorized. The repetition has been literal."

"On the other hand, your memory is faulty. I have just given a significant variant."

"Really?"

"I said ballista instead of catapult to avoid a new interruption on your part. I see the shot has backfired on me."

"What I want to know about is Nobilior's shot."

"Well, you won't."

"What, you won't finish telling me your story?"

"Yes, but there is no shot. The inhabitants of Segida surrendered at the precise moment when the ballista, all its levers bent, its elastic cords twisted taut, and its counterweight platforms filled, was ready to hurl a block of granite at them. They signaled from the walls, sent messengers, and made a pact. Their lives were spared on the condition that they evacuate the city so Nobilior might satisfy his imperial caprice of setting it afire."

"And the ballista?"

"Completely ruined. They all forgot it, including the artillery men, they were so happy at such an easy victory. While the inhabitants of Segida were signing their surrender, the cords broke, the wooden arches burst, and the powerful arm that was to launch the enormous stone remained lifeless on the ground, broken off, letting the stone roll from its fist—"

"How do you account for that?"

"But don't you know that a catapult that doesn't shoot immediately is ruined? If Professor Burns didn't teach you this I seriously doubt his competence. But let's get back to Segida. Nobilior received eight thousand pounds of silver as ransom money for the important people, which he immediately had coined to prevent the imminent uprising of his own soldiers who had not been paid.

144

Some of these coins are still preserved. Tomorrow you can see them at the Numancia Museum."

"Couldn't you get me one of them as a memento?"

"Don't make me laugh. The only individual who possesses coins of that period is Professor Adolf Schulten, who spent his life digging about in the ruins of Numancia, making surveys, and divining under the furrows in the fields the traces of military emplacements. What I can get for you is a postcard with the abovementioned coins on both sides."

"Let's continue."

"Nobilior knew how to reap great advantage from the capture of Segida, and the money that he coined bears his profile on one side and the silhouette of a ballista with the word 'Segisa' on the other."

"Why Segisa and not Segida?"

"You'll find out. A simple error on the part of the fellow who minted the coins. Those coins were much talked about in Rome, and the ballista even more. The emperor's workshops couldn't satisfy the demand of military chiefs who ordered catapults by the dozens, and each time bigger ones. The more complicated the better."

"But tell me something positive. How do you account for the difference in names if one always refers to the same apparatus?"

"Perhaps it's a matter of difference in size, perhaps the condition of the projectiles that the artillery man had at hand. Of course, the litobolas or petrarias, as their names indicate, hurled stones. Stones of all sizes. Commentators say they ranged from twenty or thirty pounds to eight or twelve hundred pounds. It seems that polibolas hurled stones too, but in the form of shrapnel, that is, clouds of shot. Etymologically speaking, the doribolas fired enormous darts, but also bundles of arrows. And the neuro-balistas, well we suppose—barrels of ignited material, burning faggots, cadavers, and great sacks of filth to make more polluted the infected air that the poor besieged wretches were breathing. I even know of a ballista that shot crows."

"Crows?"

"Let me tell you another anecdote."

"I see I've made a mistake in my archeologist and guide."

"Oh, please. It's a very nice anecdote. Almost poetic. I'll be brief, I promise."

"All right, tell it then and let's get on. The sun is setting now on Numancia."

"One night an artillery troop abandoned the largest ballista of its legion on a hill behind the village of Bures, on the Centóbriga route. You understand, I'm going back again to the second century B.C., but without leaving the region. The next morning the inhabitants of Bures, a hundred innocent shepherds, found themselves face to face with that threat which had sprung from the ground. They knew nothing about catapults, but they sniffed the danger. They barricaded themselves in their cabins for three days. As they couldn't stay there indefinitely, they drew lots to see who would go out the following morning to inspect the mysterious hulk. The lot fell to a timid, weak-spirited young fellow who gave himself up as lost. Everyone spent the night bidding him goodbye and encouraging him, but the youth trembled with fear. Before sunrise on that winter morning the ballista must have looked something like a shadowy scaffold."

"Did the young man return alive?"

"No. He dropped dead at the foot of the ballista under the charge of crows that had spent the night on the war machine and were flying away in fright—"

"Good Lord! A ballista that conquers the city of Segida without a single shot. Another that kills a young shepherd with a handful of flying shot. Is this what I'm to tell in Minnesota?"

"Say that the catapults were used for a war of nerves. Add that all the Roman Empire was nothing else but that, an enormous, complicated and clumsy war machine, filled with counteractive levers, each one stripping the force from the other. Excuse yourself by saying that the ballista is a decadent weapon."

"Do you think I'll get away with that?"

"Describe in detail the fatal high point of the ballista. Be picturesque. Tell them that being a teacher came to be extremely dangerous in Roman cities. School children inflicted real stonings on their masters, attacking them with slingshots that were a childish derivation of the warriors' hand ballistas."

"Do you think I'll be successful with that?"

"Be poetic. Refer to the touching episode during the siege of Carthage in 146 B.C., when the damsels gave up their heads of hair to take the place of horsehair needed in the making of the ballistic ropes."

"Do you think I'll be successful with that?"

"Be imposing. Speak in detail about the formation of a legionary train. Dwell on the two thousand carriages and beasts of burden, the munitions, the fortification and siege implements. Speak of the innumerable servants and slaves; criticize the ascendancy of merchants and saloon keepers, emphasize the prostitutes. Moral corruption, embezzlement, and venereal diseases will offer you generous themes. Also describe the huge portable oven all of stone, even the wheels, a product of the talents of the engineer Caius Licinius Licitus, which rolled along the road baking bread at the rate of a thousand loaves a kilometer."

"What a marvel!"

"Take into account that the oven weighed eighteen tons, and that it didn't travel more than a mile and a half a day on flat land—"

"How atrocious!"

"Stick to your purpose. Speak unceasingly of the great concentration of ballistae. Be generous in your figures; I shall give you the sources. Say that in the time of Demetrius Poliorcetes eight hundred machines were massed against a single city. The Roman army, incapable of changing, suffered disastrous delays, cut off among the hulking mass of wood of their oppressive war machines."

"Do you think I'll be successful with that?"

"End up by saying that the ballista was a psychological weapon, an idea of force, an overwhelming metaphor."

"Do you think I'll be successful with that?"

At this moment the archeologist saw a stone on the ground that seemed to him very appropriate for putting the finishing touch to his lesson. It was a thick, round rock of basalt, weighing about forty-five pounds. Digging it up with great enthusiasm, he then placed it in the student's arms.

"You're lucky! You wanted to take away a coin as a memento and look what destiny offers you."

"But what is it?"

"A valuable projectile dating from the Roman Era, undoubtedly shot from one of those machines that preoccupy you so much."

The student received the gift in some confusion.

"But are you sure?"

"Take this stone to Minnesota and put it on your lecture table. It will make a strong impression on the audience."

"Do you think so?"

"I myself will supply you with the necessary documentation so the authorities will permit you to take it out of Spain."

"But are you sure this stone is a Roman projectile?"

The archeologist's voice took on a somber, exasperated accent.

"I'm so sure of it that if you, instead of coming now, had come to Numancia some two thousand years ago, this stone, shot by one of Scipio's artillery men, would have crushed your head in."

At this forceful answer the student from Minnesota looked thoughtful, then affectionately clutched the stone against his chest. Letting go of it for one moment with one of his arms, he passed his hand over his forehead, as if wishing to erase once and for all the phantom of Roman ballistics.

The sun had now set on the arid Numatian landscape. A nostalgia for the river was shining in the dry channel bed of the Merdancho. The seraphim of the Angelus were flying in the distance over invisible villages. Master and disciple stood there motionless, made eternal by an instantaneous suspension, like two erratic blocks in the greyish twilight.

News Item from Liberia

As always occurs among women, the rumor has spread from mouth to mouth, and a legion of nervous pregnant women vainly consult circumspect doctors. The number of marriages has fallen off sharply, while the contraceptive business prospers in an alarming fashion.

Since the newspapermen were met with silence by the scientific organizations, they unfortunately resorted to interviewing the Association of Selt-taught Midwives. Thanks to its matronly president, a stout and sterile charlatan, the gossip has taken a definitely sinister turn: everywhere children are refusing to be born and surgeons cannot earn their living by performing Caesarean and Guillaumin operations. As if this were not enough, the ASM has just included in its catalogue of clandestine publications the detailed account of two midwives who fought hand to hand with a rebellious infant, a real devil who for more than twenty-four hours debated between life and death without taking into account the mother's suffering at all. Anchoring itself like a well digger on the iliac bones and holding tight to the ribs, the infant gave such a show of resistance that the women finally crossed their arms, letting it have its way—

Not surprisingly, the psychoanalysts are the only men of science to have opened their mouths: they attribute the phenomenon to a kind of collective hysteria and think that the women, and not the babies, are behaving in an abnormal fashion during childbirth. Thus they are expressing a clear censure of present-day man. Taking into account childbirth's explosive character, a psychiatrist, enchanted with life, asserts that the rebellion of the unborn, apparently without cause, is a true Infant Crusade against atomic tests. Before the mocking smile of the gynecologists, he concludes his allegation with startling ingenuity, hinting that perhaps this world we live in is not the best of all possible worlds.

A Tamed Woman

Today I stopped to contemplate this curious spectacle: in a square on the outskirts of town a dusty trainer was exhibiting a tamed woman. Though the performance was given on ground level and right in the middle of the street, the man conceded the greatest importance to the chalk circle previously traced, according to him, with the authorities' permission. Time and again he made the spectators who went across the line of that improvised circle step back. The chain leading from his left hand to the woman's neck was only a symbol, since the least effort would have been enough to break it. Much more impressive was the whip of loose silk that the trainer shook in the air without managing to make it crack.

A small monster of indefinable age completed the cast. Beating on his drum, he provided the musical background for the woman's act, which was nothing more than walking in an erect position, jumping over some paper obstacles, and solving some questions of elementary arithmetic. Each time a coin rolled on the ground there was a brief theatrical parenthesis for the public. "Kisses!"

ordered the trainer. "No, not that one. The gentleman who threw the coin." The woman didn't know who did, and half a dozen individuals allowed themselves to be kissed, their hair standing on end, amidst laughter and applause. A policeman approached saying that that was prohibited. The trainer extended a dirty paper with official stamps on it, and the policeman went off in a bad humor shrugging his shoulders.

In truth, the woman's performance was not something out of this world. But the man was infinitely patient, abnormally so. The public is always grateful for such efforts. It pays to see a flea dressed, and not so much for the beauty of the costume, but the effort it costs to put it on. I myself have spent a long time looking with admiration at a helpless fellow who did with his feet what very few people could do with their hands.

Guided by a blind impulse of solidarity, I turned from the woman and placed all my attention on the man. There is no doubt that he was suffering. The more difficult the tricks were, the harder it was for him to pretend and laugh. Each time she committed a blunder the man trembled in anguish. I sensed that the woman was not entirely indifferent to him, and that he had become fond of her. Perhaps during the years of her tedious apprenticeship. Between them a relationship existed, intimate and degrading, that went beyond that of trainer and beast. Whoever looks deeply into it will doubtless reach an obscene conclusion.

The public, innocent by nature, realizes nothing, missing the details that are obvious to an alert observer. The public admires the author of a prodigy, but his headaches or the monstrous details of his private life do not matter. It simply goes by results, and when it likes something, is not chary with its applause.

The only thing I can say with certainty is that the trainer, to judge by his reactions, felt proud and guilty. Evidently nobody could deny his merit in having tamed the woman, but neither could anyone minimize the idea of his infamy. (At this point in my meditation the woman was gamboling about like a lamb on a narrow, faded velvet carpet.)

The guardian of public order again approached to harass the trainer. According to the policeman, we were slowing down traffic, almost the rhythm of normal life. "A tamed woman? All of you go to the circus." The accused man again responded by bringing out as authorization his dirty paper, which the policeman read holding it far from him in disgust. (The woman, meanwhile, was gathering coins in her sequined cap. A few heroes allowed themselves to be kissed. Others drew aside modestly, half in dignity, half in shame.)

The representative of the authorities went away forever with a bribe gathered up by popular subscription. The trainer, with feigned jollity, ordered the dwarf to play a tropical rhythm on his drum. The woman, who was getting ready for a mathematical number, shook the colored abacus like a tambourine. She began to dance clumsily, with gestures that were not very suggestive. Her director felt himself utterly cheated, since in the depths of his heart he placed all his hopes on jail. Furious and dejected, he cursed the ballerina's slowness with angry adjectives. His false enthusiasm was contagious, and the public, some to a greater, some to a lesser degree, all applauded and swayed their bodies.

In order to complete the effect, and wishing to get out of the situation all he possibly could, the man began to beat the woman with his whip of lies. Then I realized my error. I rested my eyes on her, simply, as all the others were doing. I stopped looking at him, whatever his tragedy might be. (At that moment tears streaked down his floured face.)

I was resolved to contradict all my ideas about compassion and criticism. With my eyes searching vainly for the trainer's pardon, and before any other repentant got ahead of me, I jumped across the chalk line into the circle of capers and contortions.

Egged on by his father, the dwarf drummed in a frenzy on his instrument in a crescendo of incredible percussion. The woman, encouraged by such spontaneous company, outdid herself and had a noisy success. I kept in rhythm with her and did not falter or make a misstep in that improvised perpetual movement until the boy stopped playing.

As a finale, nothing seemed more fitting to me than to fall suddenly to my knees.

VARIOUS INVENTIONS

. . admite el Sol en su familia de oro
llama delgada, pobre y temerosa.
Quevedo

Ballad

In Zapotlán there is a plaza called Ameca, nobody knows why. A wide, cobbled street runs to its end there, then forks in two. From this point the town merges with its cornfields.

That's the little plaza at Ameca with its octagonal shape and its houses with immense doors. One afternoon a long time ago two rivals met there by chance. But there was a girl in between.

Lots of carts and wagons go through the little plaza at Ameca and their wheels grind the earth into the ruts until it becomes very fine. A fine white dust that burns the eyes when the wind blows. And there was a fountain there until recently. A water pipe with its bronze faucet and stone basin.

The girl with her red water jug arrived first along the wide street that divides in two. The rivals were walking opposite her along the side streets, not knowing they would meet at the intersection. The two men and the girl seemed to be going along, each on his own street, in accord with destiny.

The girl was going for water and she turned on the faucet. At that moment the two men saw each other and realized they were interested in the same thing. Each one's street ended there, and neither wished to go ahead. They stood there glaring fiercely at each other and neither lowered his eyes.

"Look here, friend, you're staring at me."

"Well, staring is natural."

Without speaking, that is what they seemed to say. Their looks said everything. There wasn't a word of warning. In the plaza which the townspeople were purposely deserting the thing was about to start.

The stream of water pouring into the water jug—all that broke the dead silence—was filling those two with the desire to fight. The girl turned off the faucet, realizing what was up, when the water already was spilling over. She thrust the jug on her shoulder, almost breaking into a run she was so scared.

The two men who wanted her were at the last stage of suspense, like fighting cocks not yet unleashed, hypnotized by the black points of each other's eyes. When she stepped up on the opposite sidewalk, the girl stumbled, and the jug and water came crashing down to the ground in pieces.

That was all the signal they needed. One with a dagger, a real big one, and the other with a large machete, they went at each other with their blades, parrying the blows a little with their sarapes. All that was left of the girl was the water stain, and there the two men fought for the remains of the water jug.

They were both good and they both struck home. On that afternoon that was almost over and then stopped. They both lay there, face up, one with his throat slit, the other with his head sliced open, like good fighting cocks, just one of them with a bit of breath left.

Afterwards, in the evening, lots of people came. Women who began to pray and men who probably were going to notify the law. One of the dying men was still able to say something: he asked whether the other had kicked the bucket too.

Later it was learned that there was a girl involved. And the girl with the water jug got a bad reputation over the fight. They say she never even got married. Even if she'd gone as far away as Jilotlán de los Dolores, her bad name would have followed her or probably got there ahead of her.

The Convert

Everything between God and me has been solved since I accepted his conditions. I renounce my intentions and consider that my apostolic labors are ended. Hell cannot be suppressed; any stubborness on my part will be useless and self-defeating. God was very clear and definite about this, and He wouldn't even let me get to the last propositions.

Among other charges I have taken on the duty of making my disciples turn back. Disciples on earth, you understand. Those in hell will continue waiting inexorably for my return. Instead of the promised redemption, I shall only have added a new torture for them: hope. God wanted it this way.

I must go back to my point of departure. God refuses to enlighten me and I must place my spirit on the plane where it was before it took the wrong road, that is, just before receiving minor orders.

Our colloquy has developed on the site I occupy since I was snatched from hell. It is something like a cell open to the infinite and totally occupied by my body.

God did not come immediately. On the contrary, it seemed to me an eternity that I had to wait and a feeling of unspeakable postponement made me suffer more than all the earlier tortures. Past pain in some way was a pleasing memory, since it allowed me to prove I existed and to perceive the contours of my body. There, on the other hand, I could compare myself to a cloud, to a large, sensitive island, to the outer edges of a state of less and less feeling, so that I didn't really know to what degree I existed nor at what point I communicated with nothingness.

My sole capacity was thought, ever more overflowing and powerful. In my solitude I had time to walk back and forth on numerous roads; I reconstructed imaginary buildings piece by piece; I got lost in my own labyrinth and I found the exit only when the voice of God came to look for me. Millions of ideas were put to flight, and I felt that my head was an ocean bed suddenly emptying itself.

It goes without saying that God was the one who made all the conditions of the pact and that all I could do was accept them. He did not strengthen my judgment in any way; the arbitrariness was so complete that his impartiality seemed to me a lack of mercy. He limited himself to indicating the two roads to me: begin my life anew or go back to hell.

Everyone will say that the matter wasn't worth thinking about and that I should have decided immediately. But I hesitated, full of doubts. To turn back is not so easy; it means nothing less than inaugurating a life, undoing the errors and overcoming the obstacles of a former life; this for a man who has not shown much discernment demands a serenity and a resignation that God himself finds lacking in my person. It would not be difficult to falter again and detour from the road of salavation toward the abyss.

Besides, a whole series of unendurable actions and uncounted humiliations are demanded of my future conduct; I must surrender myself and publicly clarify my new situation. Everybody, disciples and enemies, must know about it. The superiors whose authority I scorned will witness the complete demonstration of my obedience. I swear that if Fra Lorenzo was not among these persons the matter would not be so grave. But it is precisely he who must find out first and appear as the agent of my salvation. He will have the strict vigilance of my life in his charge, and each one of my actions will be laid bare before his eyes.

To return to hell is also a discouraging idea; for it is not just a matter of condemnation, but of something more fundamental: the failure of all my work. My presence in hell does not make any sense now or have any importance, for I would return powerless to convince anyone or to encourage the least hope, since God has put an end to my dreams. This, discounting the very natural circumstance that everyone in hell would feel cheated. Calling me a

phony and a traitor, they would give evil and twisted interpretations to the change in me; doubtless they would devote themselves
to martyrizing me *in aeternum* on their account—

And here I am at the edge of the abyss, exhibiting my weakest
qualities, speaking of sordid fears, emphasizing my self-love. Because I cannot forget the success I had in hell. A triumph, I venture to claim, which the apostles of the earth have not seen. It was
a grandiose spectacle, and in the center was my faith, unbreakable,
multiplied, like a shining sword in the hands of all.

I fell face forward into hell, but I did not doubt a single moment.
I was surrounded by shadowy devils, but the idea of perdition did
not deter me. Legions of men were suffering torment on horrible
machines; nonetheless, at each dreadful deed my faith responded:
God wants to test me.

The sufferings that my executioners caused me on earth seemed
to go on in the same way without interruption. God himself has
examined all my wounds and He has been unable to discern which
I got in the world and which came from diabolic hands.

I don't know how long I was in hell, but I clearly remember the
rapidity and the grandness of the apostolate. I gave myself tirelessly to the task of transmitting to others my own conviction:
we were not definitely condemned; punishment subsisted thanks
to rebellious and desperate attitudes. Instead of blaspheming, one
must give examples of sacrifice and humility. Pain would not matter and nothing would be lost by undergoing a test. All God had
to do was turn his gaze toward us to know that we understood.
The flames would fulfill their purifying work and heaven's doors
would open to the first ones pardoned.

Soon my song of hope began to progress. The wellspring of
faith began to refresh hardened hearts with a forgotten accent of
sweetness. I must truly confess that for many that meant only a
sort of novelty in the course of the cruel monotony. But even the
hardest, the most obdurate, joined the clamor. And there were

devils who forgot their condition and who resolutely joined our ranks. Surprising things were seen: condemned men who went to the oven by themselves and applied coals and searing irons against their chests, who jumped into the boiling cauldrons and drank tall glasses of molten lead with delight. Devils trembling with compassion would go to them and make them rest and call a truce in their voluntary punishment. From an abject, abysmal place, hell became transformed into a holy refuge of hope and penitence.

What will they do now? Will they have reverted to their rebellion, their desperation, or will they be waiting with anguish for my return? I have no way of knowing, unless new sins lead me there again, to a hell that I shall no longer be able to look at with enlightened eyes.

I, who rejected all human arguments, who saw God's face smiling behind all the torments, must now confess my failure. It relieves me that it was God himself who deceived me and not Fra Lorenzo. The sacrifice of recognizing him as Savior in order to sufficiently punish my vanity was imposed on me; and my pride, unbroken on the coals, will bend before his cruel eyes.

All due to the fact that I wish to live a good Christian life. A surprising thing, living like a good Christian; it brings the worst results. A blind faith offends God; He asks for a vigilant, fearful faith. I completely destroyed my will, so that instincts and virtues coursed freely through my spirit and body. Instead of dedicating myself to classification, I put all my strength in faith, making of my quietism a hidden and potent flame; and I left actions to the caprice of that obscure and universal force which moves everything that exists on earth.

This all suddenly came crashing down when I realized that the good and bad acts, which I had relegated to the depository of the general conscience—vain creation of our heretical minds—were strictly registered in my personal account. God made me admit the existence of scales and records. He pointed out my errors one by one and put before my eyes the affront of a negative balance. I have nothing in my favor except faith, a totally wrong faith, but a faith whose solvency God tried to recognize.

I realize that in my case predestination is proven, but I don't know whether I will find salvation during my new attempt. God has repeatedly strengthened my uncertainty and has cast me from his hands without a single palpable proof; I am equally upset by the various routes unwinding before my inexpert eye. Belief in human incapacity has been carefully restored; I see everything as in a dream, and among my luggage I don't carry one piece of truth.

Little by little the frontiers of my body are reduced. The vague continent is incorporating itself into the mass of my person. I feel that my skin shrouds and limits the substance that had shed itself in an orb of unconsciousness. Slowly my senses are reborn and communicate with the world and its objects.

I'm on the floor in my cell. I see the crucifix on the wall. I move a leg, I touch my forehead. My lips move; I feel the breath of life and try to articulate, to force out the terrible words: "I, Alonso de Cedillo, take back and repudiate—"

Then, through the bars I distinguish Fra Lorenzo, his lantern in his hand, watching me.

A Pact with the Devil

Although I hurried and broke into a run to get to the movie, the film had already started. In the dark hall I tried to find a seat. I sat down next to a distinguished looking man.

"Excuse me," I said to him, "but could you tell me briefly what has happened on the screen?"

"Yes. Daniel Brown, whom you see up there, has made a pact with the Devil."

"Thank you. Now I want to know what the conditions of the pact are. Could you explain them to me?"

"With pleasure. The Devil commits himself to making Daniel Brown rich for seven years. In exchange for his soul, naturally."

"Just seven?"

"The contract can't be renewed. Daniel Brown signed it with a little blood not long ago."

With this information I was able to fill in the film's plot. It was sufficient but I wanted to know something more. The helpful stranger seemed to be a man of judgment. While Daniel Brown was putting a large quantity of gold coins in his pocket, I asked him, "In your opinion, which of the two has compromised himself more?"

"The Devil—"

"How is that?" I replied in surprise.

"Daniel Brown's soul, believe me, wasn't worth much at the moment when he surrendered it."

"Then the Devil—"

"Is going to come out on the short end of the deal, because Daniel shows how greedy he is for money, you see."

Indeed, Brown was spending money hand over fist. His simple country soul was dazzled. With reproachful eyes my neighbor added, "Wait until you get to the seventh year pretty soon."

I shivered. I was sorry for Daniel Brown. I couldn't help asking, "Excuse me, but haven't you ever been poor?"

My neighbor's profile, blurred in the darkness, smiled weakly. He took his eyes from the screen where Daniel Brown was beginning to feel remorse and said without looking at me, "Do you know, I don't know what poverty is."

"If that's the case—"

"On the other hand, I know very well what seven years of being rich can accomplish."

I made an effort to understand what those years might be like, and I saw Paulina's image, smiling, in a new dress and surrounded by pretty things. This image led to other thoughts: "You said a while back that Daniel Brown's soul was worthless. How do you explain then that the Devil has given him so much?"

"That poor boy's soul can improve; remorse can make it grow," answered my neighbor philosophically, then adding maliciously, "The Devil will not have wasted his time then."

"And if Daniel repents?"

My interlocutor seemed disgusted by my pity. His mouth opened as if to speak, but there came out only a little guttural sound. I insisted: "Because Daniel Brown could repent and then—"

"It wouldn't be the first time things have gone badly for the Devil. Some men have slipped out of his hands in spite of the contract—"

"Really, that's not very honest," I said, without realizing.

"What did you say?"

"If the Devil keeps his word, all the more reason for the man to keep his," I said in explanation.

"For example—" and my neighbor made a significant pause.

"Take Daniel Brown," I answered. "He adores his wife. Look at the house he bought her. He has given his soul for love and he should keep his word."

My companion was quite disconcerted by this reasoning.

"Pardon me," he said, "a minute ago you were taking Daniel's part."

"I'm still on his side. But he should keep his word."

"Would you?"

I couldn't answer. On the screen Daniel Brown was in a gloomy state. Riches were not enough to make him forget his simple country life. His house was big and luxurious, but strangely sad. The finery and the jewels were not becoming to his wife. She seemed so changed.

The years sped by and the money poured rapidly from Daniel's hand just like seeds in former years during planting time, but now, instead of plants, sadness and remorse were growing.

I made an effort and said, "Daniel should keep his word. I would too. There's nothing worse than poverty. He has sacrificed himself for his wife and the rest doesn't matter."

"You are right. You understand because you have a wife too, don't you?"

"I would give anything so that Paulina could have everything she needed."

"Your soul?"

We were speaking in low voices. Nonetheless, the people near us seemed to be annoyed. Several times they had asked us to be quiet. My friend, who seemed very much interested in the conversation, said to me, "Why don't we go out into the lobby? We could see the film later."

I couldn't refuse and we went out. For the last time I looked at the screen: in tears Daniel Brown was confessing to his wife the pact he had made with the Devil.

I continued to think about Paulina, the desperate straits in which we lived, the poverty that she supported without complaint and which made me suffer the more. I certainly did not understand Daniel Brown, who was weeping with his pockets full of money.

"Are you poor?"

We had crossed the lobby and were entering a narrow, dark, slightly humid-smelling corridor. When he had pushed aside the worn curtain, my companion asked me again, "Are you poor?"

"Today," I answered, "the movie costs less than usual, but if you knew what a time I had deciding to spend that money. Paulina insisted that I come; arguing with her about it made me late."

"Then what do you think of a man who solves his problems like Daniel did?"

"It's worth considering. My affairs are in bad shape. People no longer dress with much care, but go about in any fashion. They mend their own clothes, clean and fix them up time and again. Paulina herself knows how to get along very well. By ingenious combinations, changes here and there, she improvises clothes; it's certainly true that she hasn't had a new dress for ages."

"I promise to be your customer," said my companion, taking pity on me. "This week I'll order a couple of suits."

"Thanks. Paulina was right when she asked me to go to the movies. When she finds this out she will be very happy."

"I could do something else for you," my new customer added, "for example, I'd like to propose a business deal to make a purchase from you—"

"Excuse me," I answered rapidly, "but we have nothing else to sell; the last things were some of Paulina's earrings—"

"Think carefully now, there is perhaps something that you are forgetting—"

I pretended to think a little. There was a pause which my benefactor interrupted with a strange voice, "Reflect now, look, there's Daniel Brown. A little before you arrived, he had nothing to sell, and nevertheless—"

Suddenly I noticed the man's face had grown sharper. The red light from a sign on the wall gave a strange, fiery brilliance to his eyes. He observed my anxiety and said with a clear, distinct voice, "My dear sir, after all this, an introduction seems unnecessary. I am completely at your service."

Instinctively I made the sign of the cross with my right hand, but without taking it from my pocket. This seemed to take away the sign's virtue, because the Devil, fixing a knot in his tie, said calmly, "Here in my wallet I have a document which—"

I was perplexed. I saw Paulina again standing at the threshold of our house in her faded, but becoming, dress just as she was when I left, her face bent and smiling, her hand hidden in the middle pocket of her apron.

Our fortune was in my hands, I thought. This evening we had scarcely anything to eat. Tomorrow there would be food on the table, and dresses and jewels and a big, beautiful house. My soul?

While I was plunged in such thoughts, the Devil had taken out a crackling sheet of paper and in his hand a needle shone. "I would give anything so that you could have everything you wanted," I had said to my wife many times. Anything. My soul? Now the one who could put my words into effect stood before me. But I kept on meditating. I was doubtful. I felt rather dizzy. Brusquely, I decided: "It's a deal. But on one condition."

The Devil, who was already trying to prick my arm with his needle, seemed disconcerted. "What condition?"

"I'd like to see the end of the film," I answered.

"But what do you care what happens to that imbecile of a Daniel Brown? Besides, that's only a story. Don't bother, just go ahead and sign. The document is all in order, all we need is your signature, here on this line."

The Devil's voice was insinuating, clever, like the sound of gold coins. He added, "If you like, I can give you an advance right now."

He seemed to be an astute businessman. I replied decisively, "I must see the end of the film. Then I'll sign."

"You give me your word?"

"Yes."

We went back to the movie. I couldn't see at all, but my guide knew how to find the two seats easily. On the screen, that is, in the life of Daniel Brown, a surprising change had come about, due to some unfathomable mysterious circumstances. There was a poor and shabby house in the country. Brown's wife was preparing the meal near the fire. It was twilight and Daniel was returning from the fields with his hoe on his shoulder. Tired, sweaty, his coarse clothing all dusty and dirty, he seemed happy, nonetheless. Leaning on his hoe, he stood near the door. His wife approached, smiling. The two of them watched the day that was gently ending, promising the peace and rest of night. Daniel looked gently at his wife, and then casting his eye over the clean poverty of the house, he asked, "But don't you miss our former riches? Don't you really need all the things we had?"

The woman answered slowly, "Your soul is worth more than all that, Daniel—"

The country fellow's face lit up, his smile seemed to spread, to fill the whole house, to come from the landscape. Music swelled up from that smile and seemed to dissolve the images little by little. Then, from Daniel Brown's poor and happy home three white letters appeared, getting bigger and bigger, until they filled the whole screen.

Suddenly I found myself without knowing how among the departing crowd, pushing, trampling, violently opening a path. Someone caught me by the arm and tried to hold me back. With a wrench I broke loose and soon was out on the street.

It was night. I started to walk fast, going faster and faster until I finally began running. I didn't turn around once or stop until I got home. I entered as calmly as I could and closed the door carefully.

Paulina was waiting for me. Throwing her arms around my neck, she said, "You seem upset."

"No, it's nothing—"

"Didn't you like the film?"

"Yes, but—"

I was upset. I put my hands over my eyes. Paulina stood there looking at me, and then, without being able to stop she began to laugh and laugh happily at me. I was confused and bewildered, not knowing what to say. In the middle of her laughter she exclaimed with a gay reproach, "Is it possible that you fell asleep?"

These words calmed me down. They pointed a way out for me. As if ashamed, I answered, "It's true. I did fall asleep."

And then, as an excuse, I added, "I had a dream and I'm going to tell it to you."

When I finished my story, Paulina told me that it was the best film that I could have told her about. She seemed happy and laughed a great deal. Nevertheless, when I was going to bed I saw how with a little bit of ashes she cautiously traced the sign of the cross over the threshold of our house.

Paul

One ordinary morning when everything appeared perfectly normal and while the hum of the Central Bank's offices spread like a monotonous downpour, Paul's spirit was visited by grace. The head cashier stopped in the middle of complicated operations and concentrated on one point in his thoughts. His spirit was filled with the idea of divinity, intense and clear as a vision, distinct as a sensory image. A strange, deep-felt joy which had touched him other times like a momentary, fleeting reflection, became pure and lasting and found its fulfillment. It seemed to him that the world was inhabited by innumerable Pauls and that in that moment all of them were converging on his spirit.

At first Paul saw God, personal and total, summing up in himself all possibilities of creation. His ideas flew in space like angels, and the fairest of all was the idea of liberty, beautiful and light. The universe, recently created and virginal, disposed her creatures in harmonious order. God had imparted stillness or movement to them, but he himself remained integral, unapproachable, sublime. The most perfect of God's works was immensely remote from him. He was unknown in the midst of his creative and all-moving power; nobody could think about him or even imagine what he was like. Father of children incapable of loving him, he felt himself inexorably alone and thought that man was the only possibility of totally verifying his reality. Then he learned that man must contain divine qualities; if the contrary were true, he would be another mute, submissive creature. And God, after a long wait, decided to live on earth; he broke up his being into thousands of particles and put the germ of all of them in man, so that one day, after covering all possible forms of life, those wandering, arbitrary parts might reunite in the original model, isolating God and bringing him back to unity. Thus universal existence would come full cycle, and the process of creation, which God undertook one day when his heart was overflowing with loving enthusiasm, would be totally verified.

There is Paul at his table, lost in the current of time, a drop of water in a centuries-old sea, a grain of sand in an infinite desert, with his grey checked suit and his artificial tortoise-shell glasses, his smooth chestnut hair divided by a small part, his hands which write impeccable numbers and letters and have never stained the pages of his book, his orderly bookkeeper's mind that attains infallible results, distributes figures in straight columns, and has never made an error. There he is bent over his table receiving the first words of an extraordinary message. Nobody knows or will ever know him, but he bears within him the perfect formula, the number that is exactly right in an immense lottery.

Paul is neither good nor bad. His acts respond to a character whose mechanism is very simple in appearance; but his elements have taken thousands of years to come together, and the way he functions was foreseen at the dawn of the world. Paul was missing in our human past. The present is full of imperfect Pauls, better and worse, large and small, famous or unknown. Unconsciously, all mothers tried to have him as a son, all of them delegated that accomplishment to their descendents with the certainty of some day being his grandmother. But Paul was conceived like an indirect and remote fruit; his mother had to die at the very moment of childbirth without knowing about him. The key to the plan of his existence was entrusted to Paul with no outward warning one morning like any other morning when work hummed along as usual in the extensive offices of the Central Bank.

When he left the office, Paul saw the world with other eyes. He paid silent homage to each of his fellow human beings, he saw men with their souls bared, like animated monstrances, and the white symbol shone in all. The exalted Creator was contained and affirmed in each of his creatures. From that day Paul judged evil in another way: as a result of an incorrect distribution of virtues, in some excessive, in others scant. And the deficient whole engendered false virtues that had all the aspects of evil.

Paul felt great pity for all those people unconsciously bearing God within them, who many times forget and deny him, who sacrifice him in a corrupt body. He saw humanity delving and searching indefatigably for the lost archetype. Each man born was a probable saviour, each dead man a formula that had failed. Humankind from the first day effects all combinations possible, tries all the doses imaginable with the divine particles which are dispersed in the world. Humanity painfully hides its failures in the earth and contemplates the renewed sacrifice of mothers with emotion. Saints and wise men restore hope; the great criminals of the universe frustrate it. Perhaps before the final discovery, the ultimate deception is waiting, and the formula for the exact opposite of the archetype must be verified, the apocalyptic beast feared over the centuries.

Paul was well aware that nobody must lose hope. Humanity is immortal because God is in it, and what is lasting in man is the very eternity of God. Great hecatombs, floods and earthquakes, war and pestilence will not be able to destroy the last couple. Man will never have but one head so that it can be struck off with one blow.

From the day of his revelation Paul lived a different life. Momentary worries and anxieties disappeared. It seemed to him that the habitual succession of days and nights, weeks and months, had ceased for him. He thought time had stopped and he was living in a single, enormous moment, large and static like an island in eternity.

He devoted his free hours to reflection and humility. Every day clear ideas came to him and his brain became filled with splendors. Without any effort on his part, the universal breath was penetrating him little by little, and he felt himself illumined and transcended, as though a great breath of spring had cut through the branches of his being. His thoughts floated at the highest levels. On the street, stirred by ideas, with his head up in the clouds, it was hard for him to remember that he was on earth. The city was transfigured for him. Birds and children brought him happy messages. Colors seemed extraordinarily vivid and as though they had only recently been applied. Paul would have liked to see the ocean and the great mountains. He consoled himself with lawns and fountains.

Why didn't other men share that supreme joy with him? From his heart Paul issued silent invitations to everybody. At times the solitude of his ecstasy bothered him. All the world was his, and he trembled like a child before the enormity of the gift; but he promised himself to enjoy it in a leisurely fashion. For the moment, he must dedicate his afternoon to that great beautiful tree, to that white and pink cloud gently circling in the sky, to the game of the blond child rolling his ball on the grass.

Naturally, Paul knew that one of the conditions of his joy was that it was a secret, untransferable joy. He compared his previous life to his present one. What a desert of barren monotony! He realized that if anyone had tried then to reveal the panorama of the world to him, he would have remained indifferent, seeing everything the same, empty and without transcendental meaning.

He did not communicate to anyone his most insignificant experiences. He lived in a benign solitude, without intimate friends, and far from his relatives. His withdrawn and silent character made reserve easy. He only feared that his face might reveal the transformation or that his eyes might betray the light within him. Fortunately nothing like this happened. At his work and at the boarding house nobody noted any change in him at all. His exterior life continued exactly as before.

Sometimes, an isolated memory of infancy or adolescence suddenly came to his mind to be included in the emerging unity. Paul liked to group these memories around a central idea that filled his spirit, and he was pleased seeing in them a sort of omen concerning his eventual destiny. Omens that went formerly unheeded because they were brief and weak, and he had not yet learned to decipher those messages sent by nature, disguised in little miracles, to the heart of each man. Now they were understandable, and Paul marked out the path his spirit would take, as though he were using little white stones. Each one recalled a happy circumstance that he would relive whenever the fancy took him.

At certain moments the divine particle seemed to take on unaccustomed proportions in Paul's heart, and he was filled with fear. He would turn to his well-tested humility, judging himself the most abject of men, the most inept bearer of God, the man widest of the mark in his interminable search.

The only thing he could desire in his moments of greatest ambition was to experience the revelation of discovery. But this seemed impossible and excessive. He saw the powerful and apparently blind impulse of humankind to sustain itself, ever multiplying its efforts, always offering a solid resistance to phenomena which threaten the course of life. That power, that triumph ever more difficult to obtain, implicitly brought hope and the certainty that one day there would exist among men the first and final being. That day the instinct of self-preservation and reproduction would cease. All living men would be superfluous and would vanish, absorbed in the all-containing being which would justify humanity, the centuries, the millennia of ignorance, vice, and searching. Humankind, freed of all its evils, would rest forever on the breast of its Creator. No suffering will have been in vain, no joy either: the sufferings and the joys will have been multiplied in a single infinite being.

This idea, which justifies all, was sometimes followed in Paul's mind by the contrary idea, and it absorbed and tired him out. The beautiful dream that he dreamed so lucidly was losing clarity, was threatening to disintegrate or become a nightmare.

Perhaps God could never recover himself and would remain forever dissolved and buried, caught in millions of jails, in desperate beings, each one of them lamenting his fraction of God's nostalgia and forever joining together to recover it, in order to recover themselves in him. But the divine essence would go on weakening little by little like a precious metal many times melted and remelted that loses itself in alloys, becoming grosser each time. God's spirit would only express itself then in the enormous will to survive, closing its eyes to the millions of failures, to the daily and negative experience of death. The divine particle would beat violently in each man's heart, knocking at the door of its jail. All would respond to this call with a desire for reproduction becoming gradually more and more sluggish and senseless, and God's integration would become impossible, because in order to isolate a single precious particle, mountains of dross would have to be reduced, and swamps of iniquity drained dry.

In these circumstances Paul was seized with despair. And from despair came the final certainty which he had tried in vain to postpone. Paul began to perceive his terrible role as spectator and realized that when he contemplated the world he was devouring it. Contemplation nourished his spirit, and his hunger for contemplation was ever greater. He did not recognize his neighbors in mankind; his solitude began to take on such proportions as to become unbearable. He looked enviously at other people, at those incomprehensible beings who know nothing and who liberally throw all their energy into mean little occupations, enjoying and suffering around a solitary and gigantic Paul, who above their heads breathed in a rare and pure air and spent his days requisitioning the wealth of mankind and keeping them from repossessing it.

Paul's memory began to turn backward rapidly. He relived his life day by day and minute by minute. He reached childhood and infancy. He continued back before his birth, and knew the life of his parents and his ancestors to the earliest roots of his genealogy, where he found his spirit again controlled by unity.

He felt capable of anything. He could remember the most insignificant details in the life of each man. He could enclose the universe in a phrase, see with his own eyes the most distant things in time and space, clasp the clouds, the trees and the stones in his hand.

His spirit collapsed, filled with fear. An unexpected and extraordinary timidity governed each of his actions. He chose exterior impassivity as an answer to the active fire which was consuming his insides. Nothing should change his life's rhythm. There were indeed two Pauls, but men knew only one. The other, the decisive Paul who could weigh humanity and pronounce an adverse or a favorable judgment, remained unknown, completely unknown in his faithful grey-checked suit, the glance of his deep-set eyes protected by artificial tortoise-shell glasses.

In his infinite repertory of human memories an insignificant anecdote which perhaps he had read in his infancy would stand out and lightly hurt his spirit. The anecdote appeared in isolation and lodged its bleak phrases in Paul's brain: in a mountain village an old shepherd, who was a stranger, managed to convince all his neighbors that he was the very incarnation of God. For some time he enjoyed a privileged situation, but then a drought came. The crops were lost, the sheep died. The believers fell upon the God and sacrificed him ruthlessly.

On only one occasion was Paul on the point of being discovered. Only once was he at his true height in the eyes of another, and in that case Paul did not conceal his condition, accepting the immense risk for an instant.

It was a beautiful day when Paul was quenching his universal thirst, walking along one of the city's main avenues. An individual suddenly stopped in the middle of the sidewalk, recognizing him. Paul felt a ray descending upon him. He stood stock still and mute with surprise. His heart beat violently, but also with infinite tenderness. He started to step forward and tried to open his arms in a gesture of protection, disposed to be identified, betrayed, crucified.

The scene which seemed eternal to Paul had lasted but a few seconds. The unknown man seemed to hesitate one last time, and then, disturbed, realizing his mistake, he murmured an excuse to Paul and continued on his way. Paul stood still for some time, filled with anguish, relieved and wounded at the same time. He understood that his face was beginning to betray him and he took extra precautions. From then on he preferred to walk alone at twilight and to visit the park during the early evening hours that were so peaceful and shadowy.

Paul had to watch each one of his acts closely and exert all his strength to suppress his smallest desires. He decided not to upset the course of his life in the slightest way nor alter the most insignificant of its phenomena. For practical purposes, he annulled his will. He tried to do nothing to verify his nature by himself; the idea of omnipotence weighed on his spirit, overwhelming him.

But all was useless. The universe was penetrating his heart in torrents, returning to Paul like a wide river that carries all the wealth of its waters back to the original spring. It did him no good to resist; his heart had fanned open like a plain and on it the essence of things was raining.

In the very excess of his abundance, in the overwhelming amount of his riches, Paul began to suffer because of the impoverishment of the world that was going to be emptied of its beings, lose its warmth and stop its motion. An overflowing sensation of pity and compassion began to invade him until it became intolerable.

Everything grieved Paul: the frustrating life led by children, whose absence was beginning to be noted already in the gardens and schools; the useless life of men and the vain importance of pregnant women who would no longer survive childbirth; the young couples who suddenly would part, their superfluous dialogue already cut short, saying goodbye without making a date for the following day. And he feared for the birds, who were forgetting their nests and flying aimlessly about, lost, scarcely sustaining themselves on a motionless air. The leaves of the trees began to turn yellow and fall. Paul shuddered at the thought that there would be no other spring for them, because he was going to nourish himself on the life of everything that was dying. Suddenly, he felt incapable of surviving the memory of the dead world, and his eyes filled with tears.

Paul's tender heart did not need to prolong the examination. Nor did he set up a trial for anyone. He decided that the world should live, and he promised to return everything he had been taking from it. He tried to recall whether in the past there had not been another Paul who plunged from the height of his solitude to lead the ocean of the world into a new, dispersed, and fugitive life cycle.

One cloudy morning when the world had already lost most of its colors and when Paul's heart shone like a coffer swollen with treasures, he decided to make his sacrifice. A destructive wind roamed the world, a kind of black archangel with wings of stormy wind and drizzle that seemed to be erasing the outline of reality, a prelude for the last scene. Paul sensed that it was capable of anything, of dissolving the trees and statues, of ripping apart the stones in structures, of bearing away on its gloomy wings the last warmth left. Trembling and unable to bear for one moment more the spectacle of universal disintegration, Paul shut himself up in his room and prepared himself for death. In some way or other, like a lowly suicide, he ended his days before it was too late and opened wide the gates to his soul.

Humanity insistently continues his efforts, after having hidden under the earth another formula that failed. Since yesterday Paul has been here again with us, in us, seeking himself.

This morning the sun is shining with a rare splendor.

Parable of the Exchange

To the cry of "I exchange old wives for new!" the merchant canvassed the streets of the town with his convoy of painted carts.

Transactions, based on inexorably fixed prices, were carried out rapidly. Those interested received proofs of quality and certificates of guaranty, but nobody had a choice. According to the merchant, his were twenty-four carat women, all blonde and Circassian. More than blonde, golden as candlesticks.

As soon as men saw their neighbor's acquisition, they ran pell-mell after the dealer. Many were ruined. Only a newlywed man

could get an even exchange. His wife was brand new and did not compare unfavorably with the exotic women. But she wasn't as blonde as they.

I was all atremble behind my window as a sumptuous cart passed by. Reclining among cushions and curtains, a woman who seemed a leopard gazed dazzlingly up at me, as from a block of topaz. Seized with that contagious frenzy, I was on the point of hurtling through the glass panes, but then ashamed, I turned away from the window to look at Sophia.

She was calm, embroidering the usual initials on a new table-cloth. Untouched by the tumult, she threaded her needle with sure fingers. Only I who know her could notice her faint, imperceptible pallor. At the end of the street the merchant made his disturbing proclamation a last time: "I exchange old wives for new!" But I stayed with my feet glued to the floor, shutting my ears to this definitive opportunity. Outside the town was all in an uproar.

Incapable of any comment, Şophia and I had supper in silence. Carrying out the plates, she finally said to me, "Why didn't you exchange me for another wife?"

I couldn't answer her and we fell more deeply into the vacuum. We went to bed early but couldn't sleep. Separated and silent, that night we played the role of stony guests.

From then on we lived in a little deserted island, surrounded by tempestuous happiness. The town seemed a chicken run infested with peacocks. Lazy and voluptuous, the new women would spend the day lolling abed. They would come out at dusk, resplendent in the setting sun, like silken yellow banners.

Not for a moment did their complacent and submissive husbands leave them. Caught in this honeyed sweetness, the men neglected their work, never thinking of tomorrow.

In the neighborhood they thought I was a fool, and I lost the few friends I had. They all believed that I wanted to teach them a lesson, giving an absurd example of fidelity. They pointed at me with their fingers, laughing, casting sly remarks at me from their richly entrenched position. They dubbed me with obscene nicknames, and I wound up feeling like a kind of eunuch in that eden of pleasures.

For her part, Sophia became more and more withdrawn and silent. She refused to go out with me in order to avoid comparisons and contrasts. What is worse, she reluctantly fulfilled her strictest marital duties. To speak truly, we both felt embarrassed by such modestly conjugal love.

Her guilty air was what offended me most. She felt herself responsible for my not having a wife like the others. From the very first she thought that her humble everyday look was incapable of erasing the tempting image I carried in my head. Before the invaders' beauty she beat a retreat to the farthest corners of mute resentment. In vain I used up all our little savings, buying her trinkets, perfumes, jewels, and dresses.

"Don't pity me!"

She turned her back on all the gifts. If I made an effort to pamper her, she would answer tearfully, "I'll never pardon you for not exchanging me!"

She blamed me for everything. I was running out of patience. Recalling the leopard woman, I wished with all my heart that the merchant would come through town again.

Then one day the blondes started to get oxidized. Our little island recovered its oasis quality, now surrounded by desert. A hostile desert, full of wild, discontented cries. Dazzled at first sight, the men had not really looked closely at those women, nor had it occurred to them to assay their metal. Far from being new, they were secondhand, thirdhand, God knows how many hands old. The merchant simply made some indispensable repairs on them, and gave them a bath of such cheap, thin-layered gold that it didn't resist the test of the first rains.

The first man to notice something odd didn't let on about it, nor did the second. But the third, a druggist, noticed one day the characteristic emanation of sulphate of copper mingled in the aromas which came from his wife. Alarmed, he examined her closely and found dark stains on her skin. Then he started to yell to high heaven.

Soon similar blemishes appeared on all the women's faces, as if an epidemic of rust had broken out among them. The husbands hid their wives' defects from each other, secretly tormented with terrible suspicions concerning their cause. Little by little the truth came out, and each one learned that he had received a counterfeit woman.

The bridegroom who had been borne along on the current of enthusiasm which the exchanges provoked fell into a profound gloom. Obsessed by the memory of a body of unequivocal whiteness, he soon gave signs of madness. One day he began removing the remaining gold on his wife's body with corrosive acids, and she was left a sorry sight, a veritable mummy.

Sophia and I found ourselves envied and hated. I thought it best to take some precautions, but Sophia was loathe to dissimilate her jubilation, and she took to going out in her best finery, sparkling in the midst of so much desolation. Far from attributing some merit to my conduct, Sophia naturally thought I had stayed with her out of cowardliness and that I had really wanted to exchange her.

Today the expedition of deceived husbands left town to search for the merchant. It was really a sad spectacle. The men shook their fists in the air, vowing vengeance. The women went about in mourning, faded and disheveled, like whining lepers. The only man who stayed home is the famous newlywed, and people fear for his sanity. Showing signs of a maniacal attachment, he now declares that he will remain faithful until death parts him from his tarnished wife, whom he completely ruined with the sulfuric acid.

I don't know what my life will be like at the side of a foolish or prudent Sophia. For the present, her admirers are absent. Now we are on a real island, surrounded by solitude on every side. Before leaving, the husbands declared that they would seek even in hell for traces of their deceiver, and in truth, they all assumed the faces of condemned men on saying this.

Sophia is not as dark as she seems. In the lamplight, her slumbering face is filled with reflections, as if light, golden thoughts of pride issued from her dreams.

Letter to a Shoemaker

Dear Sir:

As I willingly paid you the money you charged me to mend my shoes, undoubtedly you are going to be surprised at the letter I feel obliged to send you.

At first I didn't realize the disaster that had happened. I received my shoes very contentedly, predicting a long life for them, satisfied with the economy I had just realized. For a few pesos, a new pair of shoes. (These were precisely your words and I repeat them.)

But my enthusiasm ended soon. When I reached home I examined my shoes closely. I found them slightly out of shape, rather dry and hard, but I didn't want to concede too much importance to this metamorphosis. I am a reasonable person. Mended shoes have something strange about them, offering a new look, which is almost always depressing.

Here I must remind you that my shoes were not completely ruined before. You yourself sang their praises because of the quality of their material and the perfect way they were made.

You even praised the make. In short, you promised me a brand new pair of shoes.

Well then, I couldn't wait until the next day and I took off my shoes to test your promise. And here I am, with my feet in pain, writing you a letter, instead of letting you hear the violent words that my unfruitful efforts elicited.

My feet wouldn't go into the shoes. Like everyone else's, my feet are soft and sensitive. I found myself saddled with a pair of iron shoes. I don't know how or with what skills you fixed them so as to make my shoes unwearable. There they sit in a corner, winking mischievously at me with their twisted toes.

When all my efforts failed, I carefully began to consider the work you had done. I must tell you that I have had no training in repairing shoes. All I know is that there are shoes that have made me suffer and others, on the contrary, so soft and flexible, that I remember them tenderly.

The pair I gave you to mend were admirable shoes that had faithfully served me for many months. My feet felt just like a fish in water in them. More than mere shoes, they were like a part of my own body, a kind of protective wrapping that gave firmness and sureness to my step. In reality, their leather was my skin, wholesome and resistant. But they were beginning to show signs of fatigue. Especially the soles: some wide and deep worn spots made me realize that my shoes were becoming strange to my person, that they were wearing out. When I took them to you, my socks were about to show through them.

I should also mention something about the heels. I don't walk properly, and the heels gave unmistakable signs of this bad old habit that I have been unable to correct.

I was anxious to prolong the life of my shoes. This desire does not seem reprehensible to me; on the contrary, it is a sign of modesty and shows a certain humility. Instead of throwing my shoes away, I was prepared to wear them for a second period, less brilliant and luxurious than the first. Besides, this custom we modest folk have of getting our shoes repaired is, if I'm not mistaken, the *modus vivendi* of people like yourself.

I must say that my examination of your repairs has led me to very unpleasant conclusions. For example, that you do not love your line of work. If you were to put aside all resentment and come to my house and look at my shoes, you would see that I am right. Just look at the stitchings; not even a blind man could have done such a poor job. The leather is cut with inexplicable carelessness, the edges of the soles are irregular and dangerously sharp. You certainly must not have shoe trees in your shop, since my shoes are so misshapen. Remember, worn out as they were and all, they still had certain aesthetic lines. And now—

But just put your hand inside them. You will feel a sinister cavern. My foot will have to be turned into a snake in order to get in it. And suddenly you hit a bump, something like a cement block, before you reach the toe. Is it possible? My feet, Mr. Shoemaker, have the form of feet; they are like yours, that is, if you have human extremities.

But that's enough. I've already told you that you have no love for your line of work and it's true. It is also very sad for you and dangerous for your clients, who certainly do not have money to throw away.

By the way, I am not speaking with ulterior motives. I am poor, but I'm not stingy. The intention of this letter is not to request a refund of the amount I paid you for your destructive work. Not at all. I am writing you simply to exhort you to love your work. I have told you the tragedy of my shoes so that you will respect that trade that life has given you, that line of work you happily learned in your youth—Excuse me, you are still young. At least, you have time to start over again, if you have already forgotten how to mend a pair of shoes.

We need good artisans like we had in the old days who do not work just to get money from their client, but to put into practice the ideals of good workmanship. Those ideals that have been unpardonably flouted in fixing my shoes.

I should like to tell you about the artisan in my home town who repaired my shoes with dedication and care when I was a small child. But this letter isn't meant to instruct you with examples.

I just want to tell you one thing: if, instead of getting irritated, you feel something like self-reproach stirring in your heart and flowing to your hands, come to my house and get my shoes, do a second job on them, and then all will be well.

I promise you that if I can get into the shoes then, I shall write you a fine letter of gratitude, recommending you as a man who keeps his word and is a model artisan.

Your faithful servant.

God's Silence

I don't think this is usually done: leaving letters open on the table so that God will read them.

Pursued by swift-flying days, harassed by stubborn ideas, I have come to a stop tonight at the end of a dark alleyway. Night is at my back like a wall and yawning before me like an inexhaustible question. Circumstances require a desperate act and I put this letter before the all-seeing eyes. I have retreated since infancy, always delaying this moment in which I am finally caught.

I don't try to appear before God's eyes as the most troubled of men. Nothing like that. Near or far there must be others who have also been hemmed in on nights like this. But I ask: what have they done to keep on living? Have they at least come out alive from the ordeal?

I need to talk and to trust myself. Nobody is destined to receive my shipwrecked message. I wish to believe that somebody will pick it up, that my letter will not float in a vacuum, opened and alone as on an inexorable sea.

Is a lost soul a little thing? Thousands fall ceaselessly, lacking support, from the day they rise up to ask for the keys of life. But I don't want to know about them, I don't pretend that explanations of the universe have fallen into my hands. I am not going to search in this shadowy hour for what wise men and saints did not find in spaces of light. My need is brief and personal.

I wish to be good and I solicit some information. That is all. I am balanced on the dizzy heights of uncertainty, and my hand, that at last comes to the surface, does not find a fragment of rock to cling to. I don't need much, just a simple bit of information.

For some time now I have been giving a certain direction to my actions, an orientation that has seemed reasonable to me, and I am alarmed. I fear I am the victim of a mistake, because everything up to now has turned out very badly.

I feel quite cheated when I see that my attempts at kindness always produce an explosive result. My scales don't work well. There is something that clearly keeps me from choosing the ingredients which produce good. There is always something malign adhering to them, and the product explodes in my hands.

Am I unfit for the achievement of good? It would hurt me to recognize it, but I confess that I would welcome an apprenticeship.

I don't know if the same thing happens to everybody else. I spend my life courted by an affable demon who delicately suggests evil things to me. I don't know if he has divine authorization: what is certain is that he doesn't leave me in peace one moment. He knows how to make temptation unsurpassably attractive. He is clever and an opportunist. Like a magician, he elicits horrible things from the most innocent objects, and is always provided with an extensive series of evil thoughts that he projects into the imagination like rolls of film. I say in all sincerity, I never turn deliberately to evil; the devil paves the way and slants all the roads. He is sabotaging my life.

If anyone is interested, here is the first fact of my biography that I recall: one day during my early school years circumstances placed me in contact with some children who knew secret, attractive things which they related in a mysterious fashion.

Naturally, I don't count my childhood a happy one. An infantile soul that carries heavy secrets flies badly; it is a weighted angel that cannot attain the heights. My childhood days, embellished by smooth landscapes, often showed deplorable stains. The devil, with the punctual apparitions of a phantom, gave a nightmarish turn to my dreams and put a pungent and evil flavor in my childhood memory.

When I discovered that God was watching over all my actions I tried to hide the bad ones from him in obscure corners. But finally, following the example of adults, I openly displayed my secrets so that they might be examined in a trial. I knew that between God and me there were intermediaries, and for a long time I transacted my affairs through them until one bad day when my childhood was over, I tried to attend to them personally. Then problems arose which I always put off examining. I began to retreat from them, to flee from their threat. To live days and days closing my eyes, allowing good and evil to do their work jointly. Until one time, opening my eyes, I took the side of one of the two contenders locked in battle. Feeling chivalrous, I chose the side of the weaker. Here is the result of our alliance: we have lost all the battles. Invariably we emerge defeated in all encounters with the enemy; here we are retreating again on this memorable night.

Why is good so defenseless? Why does it crumble so easily? Scarcely a few hours of strength are carefully built up when a blow of a minute comes to topple over the whole structure. Every night I am overwhelmed by the ruins of a day destroyed, of a day that was beautiful and lovingly built.

I feel that some time I shall not get up again, that I shall decide to live among the ruins like a lizard. Now, for example, my hands are tired for tomorrow's work. And if sleep doesn't come, even the sleep that is like a little death, to solder the sorrowful account of this day, I shall await my resurrection in vain. I shall allow dark forces to live in my soul and push it spinning toward a swift fall.

But I also ask: can one live for evil? How do the evil console themselves for not feeling in their hearts the tumultuous desire for good? And if behind each malevolent act there lurk punishing forces, how do they defend themselves? For my part, I have always lost that battle, and bands of remorse pursue me like swordsmen to this alley of night.

Many times I have reviewed with satisfaction a certain group of well-disciplined and almost victorious acts, and the slightest recollection of the enemy has sufficed to put them to flight. I find myself obliged to recognize that many times I am good just because I don't have the proper opportunities to be bad, and I bitterly remember how far I was able to go on occasions when evil put all its attractions within my grasp.

Then, in order to guide the soul granted me, I ask in the most urgent tones for something factual, a sign, a compass.

The spectacle of the world has disoriented me. Chance flows into it and confounds all. There is no place to gather together a series of facts and to confront them. Experience always follows on the heels of our acts, and is useless as a moral.

I see men all around me leading hidden, inexplicable lives. I see children drinking in contaminated words, and life, like a criminal nurse, feeding them with poisons. I see people who dispute the eternal words, who are called the favorite and the chosen. Across the centuries one sees hordes of bloodthirsty and imbecilic people; then suddenly here and there a soul that seems stamped with a divine seal.

I look at the animals gently enduring their fate and living under different norms, the vegetables being consumed after a mysterious and vigorous life, and the hard and silent minerals. My spirit wrestles with unending puzzles, which are closed tight like seeds that sprout from an inner growth-giving sap.

I distinguish and follow the track of each one of the marks that God's hand has let fall upon the earth. I listen sharply to the formless noise of the night; I bend to the suddenly yawning silence, interrupted by a sound. I observe and try to fathom the depths, to enmesh myself, to sum myself up in everything. But I always remain isolated, ignorant, individual, always on the shore.

From the shore then, from the pier, I send this letter that will be lost in silence—

Indeed, your letter has been lost in silence. But it happens that I was there at that moment. The galleries of silence are very extensive and I had not visited them for a long time.

From the beginning of the world all those things have terminated here. There is a legion of angels who specialize in bringing all the messages from earth. After they have been carefully classified, they are placed in filing cabinets distributed all through silence.

Don't be surprised that I am answering a letter which according to custom should have been deposited in silence. As you yourself have requested, I am not going to place in your hands secrets of the universe, but I shall give you a few useful pointers. I believe you will be sufficiently sensible not to conclude that you have me on your side, nor is there any reason for you to start acting, from tomorrow on, like one enlightened.

For the rest, my letter is written with words, obviously human material, and my intervention leaves no trace in them. Accustomed to managing more spacious things, these little signs, slippery as pebbles, are rather inadequate for me. To express myself properly, I should employ a language conditioned to my substance. But then, we would return to our eternal positions and you would not understand. So then, don't look in my phrases for unusual attributes: they are your very words, uncolored and naturally humble, that I utilize without experience.

There is an accent in your letter which pleases me. Used to hearing only recriminations or appeals, I find your letter has struck a note of novelty. There is nothing new in it, but it does have sincerity. The voice of a grieving son and a lack of arrogance.

Understand that men address me in two ways: sometimes with the ecstasy of a saint, sometimes with the blasphemy of the atheist. To reach me, most of them also use a stilted language of mechanical prayers that generally are empty of meaning, except when a soul that has been moved cloaks them in a genuine emotion.

You speak calmly. The only thing you might be reproached for is that you have said with so much formality, as if you knew it beforehand, that your letter was going to go unanswered. It was just chance that I was there when you had finished writing. If my visit had been a bit late, when I had read your passionate words, perhaps not even the dust of your bones would still exist on earth.

I want you to see the world as I contemplate it: like a grandiose experiment. Up to now the results are not very clear, and I confess that men have destroyed much more than I had supposed they would. I don't think it would be hard for them to finish off everything. This, thanks to a little liberty badly employed.

You scarcely touch on problems that I examine thoroughly and with bitterness. There is the unhappiness of all men, children, and animals that seem so like children in their purity. I see children suffer and I would like to save them forever, to keep them from growing up to be men. But I must wait a little longer and I wait confidently.

If you, too, can't endure the sliver of liberty you have, change the attitude of your soul and be passive and humble. Accept with feeling what life places in your hands and don't try for celestial fruits; don't go so far.

Regarding the compass you ask for, I must make clear to you that I have placed one somewhere, and I cannot give you any other. Remember that I have already given what I could to you.

Perhaps it would be good for you to find repose in some religion. This I leave to your judgment too. I cannot recommend any of them to you, because I am the last person who should do so. Anyway, think about it and decide if there is a strong voice within you demanding religion.

What I do recommend to you very strongly is that instead of occupying yourself in bitter investigations, you devote yourself to observing the small cosmos that surrounds you. Carefully register the daily miracle and take beauty to your heart. Receive its ineffable messages and translate them into your tongue.

I think you need activity and that you still have not understood how deeply important work is. You should look for some occupation that would satisfy your needs and leave you only a few free hours. Pay the greatest attention to this; it is a bit of advice that will do you lots of good. After a day's hard work, one doesn't often experience nights like this, which fortunately you have just been passing through in deep sleep.

In your place, I would look for a gardener's post or cultivate a garden patch of my own. With the flowers in it and the butterflies that would come to visit them, you would have enough to make your life happy.

If you feel very lonely, search for the company of other souls and frequent them, but don't forget that each soul is especially constructed for solitude.

I should like to see other letters on your table. Write me, if you give up dealing with disagreeable things. There are so many topics to talk about, that surely in your lifetime you will only manage to discuss very few of them. Let us select the most beautiful subjects.

Instead of signing this letter, and so you will know it is real and that you are not dreaming, I am going to offer you something: I am going to appear before you during the day in such a way that you will easily recognize me. For example— But no, you alone will have to discover how.

The Fraud

From the date of Mr. Braun's death the Prometeo stoves inexplicably began to give trouble. A smell of gas would fill the kitchens, and the stoves, gone out and smoking, would refuse to function. Accidents occurred: warehouses burned and pipes exploded. The alarmed technicians at the Braun factory began to search for the causes of this phenomenon. They thought up new improvements, but they came up with these too late. In the general disorder, a competitive firm got control of the stove market, rapidly brought about Prometeo's bankruptcy, and buried its prestige in an uproar of bloodthirsty publicity.

The people involved in this matter think I am chiefly to blame. Furious creditors, in front of the whole office force, denounced my activities, speaking of fraud and placing my honor in question. This is all because I was the last one to jump into the sinking boat and because I gave the final orders to the confused crew.

Yesterday I found myself for the last time before the group

of bookkeepers and notaries who were liquidating the bankrupt business. I had to undergo a minute investigation concerning all my personal affairs. And naturally, my "little" economies were brought up. I use quotation marks to indicate how this word was stressed by one of the scribes. I almost struck him, but contained myself and shut him up with figures. I spoke of extra wages, bonuses, and of the one percent of the sales volume of the Braun firm which I received in addition. The man was more convinced by my violence than by the force of my reasoning. I don't care.

Speaking with all justice, the failure of the Braun firm is a lamentable sequence of failures, among which mine stands at the very front. The last phase of this commercial fight was a duel between advertisers, and I lost. I know very well that our adversary was using illicit weapons, and it is easy to demonstrate that fifty percent of the disaster was due to a fine job of sabotage, directed by our competitors and executed by a group of unfaithful employees whom I can name. But I am not anxious to recover what was lost. The profound change in my spirit makes all clarification unnecessary. Why not say it? I feel somewhat removed from the world.

It was imperative to defend my honor and I have managed to do so. That's enough. But the worst part is that those famous savings have become unbearable. Any reasonable person would affirm that they legally belong to me; nonetheless, I don't see this very clearly with my new outlook. Mr. Braun made his money constructing and selling stoves; I made mine convincing the public that they should buy them. I proclaimed their quality to the four winds and I managed to raise the brand of Prometeo to heights that amazed even Mr. Braun. Now that prestige has collapsed; numerous people have suffered considerable losses, and everyone complains while I conserve my booty intact. The money, kept in a safe deposit box at the bank, weighs on my conscience.

Thoughts of my guilt, attacking me more intensely all the time, have crumbled the last defenses of my ego. Of course, it would be very easy to get rid of the money by throwing it to that handful of imbeciles who were critical of my management, but I sincerely believe that I must not spend it foolishly by giving lessons to idiots. I have found something better. It seems to me a good idea to make some clarifications.

In another era I would have been a minstrel, a beggar, a teller of tales and miracles. I discovered my vocation too late, having reached maturity in the middle of a century in which these people do not fit. Anyway, I have wished to tell my fable to two or three people who are poor in spirit, to offer my miserable collection to some naive folks who are behind the times.

I know there have been many men who have suddenly become transformed for good or bad. They lived in disguise most of their lives and one day, to everyone's astonishment, they showed themselves to be saints or devils in their true form. Naturally, I cannot aspire to a metamorphosis of this kind; nonetheless, I recognize that in my attitude a little bit of the supernatural is at work. After all, the absurd impulse that moves me to get rid of a fistful of money could convert itself into the superior energy that might generate other actions of a higher nature. All I must do is speed up the rhythm of certain thoughts and let them reach their final consequences. But—

I am like a stove that functions badly; ever since Mr. Braun's death, I have had scruples and felt remorse. From that date, an obscure and complicated anxiety has taken hold of me. A hidden sap has stirred in my deepest roots, tormenting me with a desire for inner renewal, impossible as this is. Weak sprouts trying to push up through a hard outer bark.

I live, thanks to my memories. Rather, my memories impose themselves on me like dreams, leaving me confused and sorrowful. I have the impression that a drug, taken who knows when, has stopped working. My conscience, no longer anesthetized, gives itself over to childish imagination. It is difficult for me to close the door on these things: a Christmas night filled with sounds and brilliant lights, a favorite toy, a clear, sunny day when I was running through the country—

All this had its origin on that memorable day when I opened the door of his office and found Mr. Braun slumped over his desk, showing no signs of life. Confused and rapidly passing days followed afterwards. The ruin of the business, the scandal of the bankruptcy fell on me like a rain of rubble. The errors and complaints, the discontent and claims were having a powerful effect on my spirit. Unconsciously, I placed myself in the forefront, I assumed a mask of responsibility, and contributed to the failure by investing large sums of money in a publicity campaign as useless as it was expensive. Mr. Braun did not die suddenly. We called in all the aids of science for him, which only succeeded in adding two hours of agony to his life. I shall never forget those two interminable hours which belong to eternity, or the image of Mr. Braun, choking to death. He was surrounded by stenographers, doctors, dismayed employees, and attended by a priest who mysteriously appeared out of nowhere, and, in the confusion, managed to put the terrified dying man's affairs in order, while Mr. Braun was murmuring incoherent phrases having more to do with the future disaster of the Prometeo stoves than with his soul.

A second injection produced only a period of convulsions which got gradually weaker and weaker. The doctors abandoned their task, realizing that death was taking over the office of Mr. Braun. I was so upset that I received some medical aid to prevent a possible crisis. Curiously, at the most acute moment of my shock, standing before my employer's body, I could only summon a childish response from my businessman's repertoire: I remembered the end of a half-forgotten prayer and I put my hands to my face in the gesture of a vague cross.

Like all magicians, Mr. Braun took his secret formula to the tomb. I had witnessed the development of his business affairs and helped him as his closest and chief employee. But I always waited in vain for him to let me in on the secret of his combination. This perhaps would have allowed me to carry out the firm's affairs. But I never got past the rank of helper. This word seems a good choice to me, because Mr. Braun exercised a sort of priesthood within the materialist religion that proclaimed man's happiness on earth. His personal contribution to human comfort was the Prometeo stove, and its models, following the rhythm of progress, were improved each year. He preached that the home was a paradise, modest and frugal, in which the stove held the rank of altar, in a kitchen clean and pleasing as a temple.

I was the loudspeaker for his sermons, the industrious secretary who kept track of his daily successes, the author of circular letters bearing the good tidings to housekeepers and sweating, black-smudged cooks kneeling before their millennial ovens.

Despite his high position, Mr. Braun liked to go back to the early days. From time to time he abandoned the sumptuous office to go sell a stove personally, like a dignitary descending from his chair to help a humble person. His gestures then were grave and solemn. Slowly he would carry the gas siphon and turn on the burners while he spoke with emotion about the modern gas system, guaranteed not to have bad odors or accidents. When he put a lighted match close to the burner, his face took on an anxious expression, lightly colored with fear, as if the idea of a failure upset him momentarily. When the little blue flame grew, Mr. Braun displayed a beatific smile that covered and dissipated all the client's doubts.

Recalling these scenes, I still believe, despite ruin and discredit, that Prometeo stoves are good, and because of this conviction I am ready to sacrifice all I possess. If the stoves are no good, I can do nothing; I will calmly abandon the cause and leave the utilities in other.cleaner hands. My procedure is simple and its efficacy is beyond doubt: "Out-of-order Prometeo stoves bought," and immediately following, my name and address. I shall publish this ad tomorrow in a daily paper.

I am playing heads or tails. I am betting against the majority opinion. Let the notaries and victims come now and say I am a phony.

I think happily that my gesture constitutes the best homage that can be paid Mr. Braun's memory.

I have let quite a little time go by without deciding to add these lines. I don't know how to do it; I feel somewhat inhibited by the events that have transformed my life. When I mention a clear and natural fact, I have the impression that I am going to pull a trick for the first time.

The ad published in the daily paper had a frightening result. After two days I had to provisionally suspend buying stoves because I didn't have any place to put them. They were even under the bed at my house. My savings were seriously affected.

When I had decided not to buy another stove a lady dressed in black arrived with little Arthur by the hand. A cart was following her, bringing a stove big as a piano. It was one of those Prometeo family stoves, the pride of the Braun firm, equipped with eight burners, a pastry oven, an automatic water heater, and I don't know how many other things. Discouraged, I put my hands on my hips, and in that belligerent attitude a decisive turning point overtook me.

The lady and I only needed to exchange the necessary words about the stove. In any case, we used a thousand commonplaces to sustain an ordinary conversation. But mysteriously, we got off the track. Along the wide road of trivial, ordinary words, following a simple question-and-answer method, we came to a cliff. We suddenly launched, with a minimum of words, into one of those comedies, those masterpieces of chance that life can improvise anywhere.

Our situation became unbearable because of its naturalness: we were three converging people and an imperious destiny took hold of us, disposed to lead us to an inescapable end. I felt myself guided and counseled, while I fashioned and riveted links, innocent phrases that bound us together like chains.

In reality, I knew by memory what I was saying. I was representing myself and I had not done it before because nobody had given me the right reply, which would set off the mechanism of my soul.

Fortunately, we very soon understood that our two parts formed a perfect dialogue and that it wasn't necessary to continue to the end. We would have time for that. What shortly before had seemed strange, difficult, impossible, became the most simple and natural of possible things.

Now I bear the responsibility of others' lives on my back. Mr. Braun's phantom has stopped pursuing me. Clear faces now occupy the place of former clouds. Beneath the burden I feel myself walking lightly, in spite of my forty years.

The Crow Catcher

Crows take recently planted corn from the earth. They like the tender stalks too, those three or four little leaves that are scarcely out of the ground.

But it is very easy to frighten crows. There are never more than three or four of them in all the pasture, and they can be seen from far away. Hilario makes them out among the furrows and

lets fly a stone at them with his slingshot. When one crow flies away, the others fly off too, cawing with fright.

But who sees gophers? They are the color of the earth. Sometimes you think they are a lump of earth. But then the earth moves, runs, and when Hilario raises the shotgun, the gopher is already deep down in his hole. Gophers gobble up everything— the seed grain, the small shoots of corn, and the large; the tender ears and even the ripe ears. They are troublesome all year long. They have two pouches, one on each side of the chest, and there they store everything they steal. Sometimes during harvest one can kill them with stones, because they have stuffed an ear of corn in each pouch and can scarcely move.

To spy on gophers you have to wait by their hole with your gun well loaded. After awhile they stick out their heads and seem to be laughing, showing their long yellow teeth. You must hit them right in the head so they will be really dead without moving. For a gopher that gets into his hole is a lost gopher. Not because he doesn't die, for it doesn't make any difference, but because Hilario can't cut off his tail then.

Gopher hunters are paid daily according to the number of tails they turn in to the boss every night. Before, they used to pay ten centavos for them. If you killed five or six you did pretty well. But you have to take into account the powder and ammunition. In addition to the shots that miss and the gophers that get inside their holes, every night you have to deliver at least ten or twelve tails. When it has gone very badly for the gopher hunter and he doesn't get even one tail, the boss gives him twenty-five centavos for getting rid of the crows.

"I assure you, Don Pancho, that I killed about a dozen. But there are some real tough ones; even though I hit them a good one on the head, they still slip away from me."

"How many tails shall I put down for you, Layo?"

"Just imagine, Don Pancho, I killed about twelve. I almost felt like getting down to dig for them—"

"But how many tails did you bring in?"

"Only four, Don Pancho."

"Well, then that's forty centavos, Hilario. Shall I put it down for Saturday or do you want your money now?"

"Oh, better give it to me now."

"Ten, twenty, thirty, forty, Layo. Let's see if you can do better tomorrow. Get them right in the head. Good night."

Forty centavos went quite a long way when a half liter of alcohol cost ten centavos. When you've spent all day out in the hot sun killing a dozen gophers and they only pay you for four, you feel like having a drink, if only not to hear what the old woman's going to say. Because if you go home with forty centavos, well, there's always an argument and this way, you might as well get hung for a sheep as a lamb."

"Come on, Tonino, pour me out a drink for five centavos, but make it a good one, for I need it."

"Hey now, Layo, you going to leave me here just watching?"

"Make it two instead of one, Tonino. Well, what do you say, Patricio, how did you make out?"

"Oh, the same old thing, Layo. How many did you kill today?"

"Son of a bitch—I killed about twelve and most of 'em got away."

"Didn't you hit them all right?"

"Didn't I hit them— Right in the noggin, but you know, Patricio, gophers are tougher than cats. Hey, Tonino, bring us two more, but put something in them, man, these don't have any zip."

"Layo, you really are a fool. Me, too, you know I was a gopher killer for Don Pancho and I didn't even make enough for tortillas. But then I found the way to fix the old man—"

"How'd you do it?"

"Oh, it was nothing, I just went to Espinosa's ranch, along El Camino del Agua. There's a whole colony of gophers there; I killed about twenty and then I charged Don Pancho for them like they were from his pasture."

"You don't mean it."

"Oh, the old man was really pleased. He sure was! He put the whole row of little tails on the table and he said to me: 'Now we're finishing off these sons of guns. Give it to them, Patricio. Bring me every last tail, even if you leave me without a nickel'."

"Without a nickel, why the old beggar— But if I took him all the gophers, I don't mean the Espinosa ranch ones, but all the ones on the plain, it wouldn't put a dent in his pocketbook, even if he paid me a peso for each one. It wouldn't make any difference to him."

"Hey, Tonino, this isn't making us drunk at all. Bring two more, but don't spill any now. Put in the stuff that really has some punch or we'll go to El Guayabo."

"Here they are, Layo, and that's thirty centavos for six drinks."

"Look, Tonino doesn't trust me. Who told you I wasn't going to pay?"

"Come on and pay, pay up, and don't talk so much."

"Well, here's forty all at once, so you can bring two more, but see you don't forget—"

"Listen, Layo, where do you think we are? At the fireworks factory? Get out your cigarettes—"

"Well then, why did you quit the gopher-killing game?"

"Why, brother, the old man found out where the tails were coming from and he gave me the sack."

"How'd he find out?"

"Well, Espinosa's gopher hunter, who got along fine with me, got mad one day and said that I was probably killing off all the gophers, that they were getting terribly shy, and that he wasn't killing hardly any. And he must have opened up and told on me, because the next day, well I better not tell you about it. The old man got black with rage and even wanted to throw me in the jug."

"And what happened?"

"Just think, Espinosa's sharecropper paid Don Pancho for the tails I had sold him. And I don't doubt for one minute that Don Pancho charged him too much, because that old bastard never misses a chance to pick up an extra penny."

"And what you going to do now?"

"Well, brother, I'm making adobes, what else could I do? I sure don't like it much. Up there with Don Tacho above La Reja—on the slope of the hill—"

"Well, I think it's probably better anyway to work on the adobe job. At least there you've got the damned mud and all you got to do is just keep at it. While gophers, those bastards, some days don't even come out when you call them sons of bitches."

"Well, if you want to pick up some dough, leave Don Pancho and come to La Reja tomorrow. You can see the adobe works from there—"

"But I don't know how to make adobe."

"Well, you can put 'em in the wheelbarrow, anybody knows how to carry things. Or you can work at the mixing, just as you like."

"Okay, then I'll see you early tomorrow."

"What's all this commotion and what are all these people doing here, mamma, it seems like a wake!"

"Good heavens, Layo, don't say that. Can't you hear the baby crying?"

"You mean to say it was born?"

"Hush, she got very bad with fever. If it wasn't for Doña Cleta who was here all day, you wouldn't have seen her alive."

"And what was it?"

"A boy, but he was born with his navel torn."

"Well, let them cure him."

"They already put a little lard with lime and sugar on him, for it's awfully good for anything swollen."

Hilario's wife is like dry earth just before it rains. She pays no attention to anything. The baby cries and cries. Doña Cleta said they better talk to the doctor if he keeps on crying tomorrow. For her part, she did all she could. The child was also born with his eyes half-blinded, they seem to be stuck together. Hilario's mother says they must call the doctor too.

"Well, mamma, take the shotgun tomorrow and pawn it at Tonino's, he'll surely give you five pesos."

"The shotgun? And how will you get the gophers, Layo?"

"Gophers? What are you talking about? That's finished. I sure wish the gophers and crows would eat up all Don Pancho's grain, the old so and so. I work my head off day after day killing gophers without any tails, and what's the difference whether they have tails or not when you don't get paid for them?"

"And what are we going to do then, Layo?"

"Tomorrow I'm going to stick adobes together with Patricio at Don Tacho's adobe works up there at La Reja."

"But you don't know how to make adobe, Layo."

"Well, to put the mix in the wheelbarrow you don't have to know how, or to mix the mud either. And I'm not so dumb. Making adobes is sure better than sitting in the sun watching for gophers. To hell with the gophers!"

The rain that comes from the direction of Las Peñas means a sure storm. If it comes from Santa Catarina, it probably won't amount to anything. But the rain from Las Peñas is always the real thing. Las Peñas mountain is up against the sky. And the wind pushes the clouds from behind to the other side of the mountain until they pile up and suddenly appear above the cliffs like a black puff of smoke, thundering and somersaulting over the town.

People know this, and when they see that the rain is coming from Las Peñas, they scurry about everywhere. In a moment it starts pouring down in buckets, as if the clouds just broke apart, and the water pouring in great streams.

Well, the people run to take shelter and that's it. But the adobes? Who would go get the adobes, recently made and still quite wet? It's been three days now that the water comes pouring down consistently about four in the afternoon from Las Peñas.

Now the storm is right over the adobe racks, crumbling them with its pounding torrents of water. The adobes are all squashed flat and the place where they are baked in the sun has become a mudhole.

"But what damn bad luck, who in the hell has the bright idea of making adobes during the rainy season!"

Layo gazes, shaking his head. His back aches from too much wheelbarrow. The adobes are no longer in the form of adobes. They look like cow pies.

"Patricio, I'm really in a bad way now! You didn't tell me that the adobe business could get fouled up too—"

"Wait 'til Don Tacho comes to see what he'll say. The water has been messing up our adobes for three days now."

Don Tacho arrived just about sundown.

"Well, boys, things are really bad. We'd better let this adobe making wait until we get a little summer. If we keep on we'll tempt the patience of God. Three days of continuous rain and all your work for nothing. Go to the store tonight and you'll get your bit of pay. You see the adobes that were dried out best hardly stood up under the drenching—"

Hilario and Patricio leave without a word, trudging along street after street until they reach the plaza.

"Layo, this was a terrible blow. We'll have to go back to working on the plain."

"But where are we going to find work, because they've got plenty of help everywhere. There's no chance with Don Pancho because Tonino has my shotgun."

"Did you tell Don Pancho you were going to pawn it?"

"What the hell do you mean, tell him? You crazy? I just up and cleared out, that's all."

"And how much did Tonino loan you then?"

"Five pesos, that's all. And they were spent on the kid who didn't get any better and who hasn't stopped yelling since he was born."

"Well, you'll see, Layo, five pesos isn't much. Let's go to Tonino's and ask him to give us two drinks, so we won't have any bad effects from the soaking we got; you know we were pretty warm when the downpour began."

Tonino was a good sport. They didn't get just two or even three drinks. After all, this Patricio has some good ideas. The Espinosa ranch gophers and other even more curious things. What always happens is they take him off to jail every now and then. Then he has to go back to making adobes to get back on his feet. Because with adobes there's no way of cheating. Dig up the mud, then mix it well so there won't be any lumps in it. Cart it in the wheelbarrow, and that's all. Of course, then you have to know how to mold. Wet down the adobe mold so the adobe won't stick to it. Then fill up half of it with mud, and throw a handful of pine needles in to hold it together, then fill the mold up to the top so it will stick together. Finally you smooth it down and the adobe is finished.

When Hilario and Patricio went to Don Tacho's store, Don Tacho was right in not wanting to pay them.

"Come back tomorrow, boys, and get as drunk as you like. That's enough drinking you've done for now. Better go sleep it off."

"There's a wake this time, Layo. Ugh, how drunk you are, son! What's got into you? Just think, Doña Cleta hardly had time to pour the water on the little angel, so he wouldn't go to limbo."

There was the child laid out on a small table among wild yellow and red carnations, clad in a crepe-paper dress with a tiny tinsel cross on his forehead.

Hilario's wife sat dazed in a corner. You couldn't tell whether or not she was weeping. Women came in and out bringing flowers for the little angel. Hilario, tired out and dead drunk, stretched out on the floor and soon was snoring.

The tallow candles went out at midnight. Then Hilario's wife began to cry very hard in her corner. Not so much for the child, for God had taken him, but because there were no more candles for keeping watch over him, and she felt bad for her little angel there in the darkness.

Don Tacho heard about the child and he gave Hilario two extra pesos to buy the coffin. Hilario bought a small blue box, as small as a shoe box. It was adorned with some ordinary little pebbles and on top of the lid was a little tinfoil angel with open wings.

Hilario went to the graveyard in the afternoon with the box under his arm. There he quarreled with the gravedigger because he dug such a shallow grave, only about a foot and a half deep. Hilario took the spade and there he was digging away until the sun went down.

This was in the times when everything was dirt cheap, when the peons made sixty centavos a day at their jobs and when gophers' tails brought ten centavos each. The boy who was crow catcher got twenty-five centavos for scaring off the crows all day long with his slingshot.

Hilario's child was born and died during planting time. When the crows swoop about over the pastureland and look among the furrows for tender cornstalks that have just come out of the ground, shining like tiny green stars.

Private Life

The only condition made for publication of this story is that I change the two names appearing in it, a requirement easily explained, since I am going to speak of something that has not happened yet and that I hope to influence.

As readers will realize immediately, I am referring to that love story circulating among us in versions which are getting more cruel and nasty every day. I have proposed to dignify it by telling it just as it is, and I shall be satisfied if I manage to remove all ideas of adultery from it. I write this horrible word without trembling, because I am sure that many people will concur with me in dismissing it in the end, once they have considered two things that everyone now seems to forget: Teresa's virtue and Gilbert's chivalry.

My story is the last attempt to honestly resolve the conflict that has broken out in a home in this town. For the present, the author is the victim. Resigned to such a difficult situation, he beseeches the heavens that nobody should substitute for him in this role and that he be left alone facing the general incomprehension.

When I say I am the victim I am just following the current opinion. Deep down inside I know that all three of us are victims of a cruel fate, and I shall not place my anguish above theirs. I have seen Gilbert and Teresa suffer close at hand; I have also contemplated what could be called their happiness, and I found it painful, because it is guilty and hidden, though I am prepared to thrust my hand into the fire to prove their innocence.

It has all taken place before my very eyes and the rest of society too, that society which now seems to be indignant and offended, as if it knew nothing. Naturally, I am not in a position to say where a man's private life begins and where it ends. Still, I can affirm that each one has the right to take things the way he wishes and the right to resolve his problems in the manner he judges most appropriate. The fact that I am the first here to open the windows of my house and publish this affair should not surprise or alarm anyone.

From the first moment when I realized that Gilbert's friendship was beginning to create gossip because of his constant visits, I took a line of conduct which I have faithfully followed. I proposed to hide nothing, to bring the matter out into the open so that no shadow of mystery would fall upon us. Since it was a question of a pure feeling between honorable persons, I dedicated myself to showing it loyally, so that it could be examined on all sides. But that friendship, which my wife and I equally enjoyed, began to take on a special tone and aspect which I would be very foolish to hide. I realized this from the beginning, for contrary to what people think, I have eyes in my head and I use them to see what is going on around me.

At first Gilbert's friendship and affection were directed exclusively toward me. Later, they went beyond me and lodged in Teresa's soul. I noted happily that such sentiments found an echo in my wife, who up until that time had kept herself slightly aloof, indifferently watching the play and outcome of our frequent chess matches.

I realize that more than one person would like to know exactly how things started and who, obeying a fatal sign, was the first to put the intrigue into motion.

The pleasant circumstance of Gilbert's presence in our town was simply due to the fact that after he had finished a brilliant career as a lawyer the authorities named him as Judge of Letters on one of our local courts. Though this occurred at the beginning of last year, it was not duly appreciated until the sixteenth of September, when Gilbert was to make the official speech honoring our heroes.

That speech has been the cause of everything. The idea of inviting him to eat came to me there at the Plaza de Armas amid the popular enthusiasm Gilbert elicited so admirably. Here in Mexico patriotic fiestas are just an annual pretext for having a good time and carrying on in the name of Independence and its heroes. That night the skyrockets, the commotion, and the campaign seemed for the first time to make sense and were the appropriate and direct continuation of Gilbert's words. Our national colors seemed again to be dyed in the blood, faith, and hope of all. That night in the Plaza de Armas we were indeed all members of the large Mexican family, and we felt happy and were moved like brothers.

Back home, I spoke for the first time to Teresa about Gilbert, who as a boy had known an orator's success, reciting poems and little speeches at school festivals. When I told her I had thought about inviting him to dinner, she agreed with such indifference that now I am filled with emotion.

The unforgettable night when Gilbert dined with us does not seem to be over yet. It became multiplied in visits and conversations, it had all the coincidences which heighten great friendships, it knew the joy of memories and the intimate pleasure of confidences. Unknowingly it led us to this blind alley where we now are.

Those of you who had a favorite friend at school and who know from experience that such friendships do not usually survive childhood days, the intimate relationship becoming gradually more and more difficult and cold, will well understand the satisfaction I felt when Gilbert recalled our former camaraderie in a sincere and affectionate manner. I who had always felt slightly humiliated before him, because I had stopped studying and had to stay here in this town, stagnating behind a clothing-store counter, finally felt myself justified and redeemed.

The fact that Gilbert spent the best of his free hours with us, though he had all the social distractions within reach, did not cease to flatter me. Of course, I got a little uneasy when Gilbert, so that he would feel freer and more at ease, put an end to a courtship that seemed quite serious and for which everyone had predicted the usual outcome. I know there were evil-minded people who judged Gilbert's actions to be equivocal, but he seemed to prefer friendship to love. In the light of present circumstances, I feel I cannot deny the prophetic value such gossip had.

Fortunately, an incident occurred then that I judged completely favorable, since it gave me the opportunity to get this kernel of drama out of my home temporarily.

Three respectable ladies presented themselves at my house one night when Gilbert was not there. Of course, he and Teresa were in on the secret. It simply was a question of asking my permission for Teresa to play a role in an amateur drama.

Before we got married Teresa frequently took part in such plays and came to be one of the best of the group that was now begging for her services. She and I had agreed that that diversion was completely over with. More than once, indirectly, Teresa had received invitations to act in various parts which were fitting for her new situation as housewife. But we always refused.

I never forgot that the theatre meant a great deal to Teresa and her natural gifts contributed to this feeling. Whenever we attended the theatre, she assigned a role to herself and enjoyed it as if she were truly playing the part. Once I told her that there was no reason she should deprive herself of this pleasure, but she stuck to our agreement.

Now since I had the first hint of what was going on, I took a different stand, but I let them ask me so as to justify myself. I left to the good ladies the task of convincing me of each and every circumstance that made my wife's acting indispensable. The decisive fact was left until the last: Gilbert had already agreed to play the role of the gallant. Really there was no reason for me to refuse. If the most serious objection was that Teresa would play the role of a young lady, the matter lost all importance if her partner was a friend of the family. I finally gave my permission. The ladies expressed their personal thanks to me, adding that people would be very grateful for my attitude.

Shortly afterwards, Teresa thanked me, a little shamefacedly. She too had a personal motive: the drama she was going to play in was nothing less than *The Return of the Crusader*, which in her unmarried days she had rehearsed three times without its ever being performed on stage. In reality, Griselda's role was in her heart.

I felt relieved and contented at the idea that now our dangerous evenings were going to be momentarily suspended in favor of rehearsals. There we would be surrounded by numerous people, and the situation would no longer have the suspicious characteristics that were beginning to appear.

As the rehearsals took place in the evening, it was very easy for me to leave the store a little before my usual hour to join Teresa at the home of a respected family who had thrown open their house to the group of amateurs.

My relief did not last long. As I have a clear voice and read well, the director of the group asked me one night, with a fear of offending me that was touching, to be the prompter so that I wouldn't be bored. The proposal was made half-seriously and half in jest, so that I could answer without rebuffing him. As you would suppose, I accepted enthusiastically and the rehearsals continued. Then I began to see clearly what had only been before a vague apprehension.

I had never seen Gilbert and Teresa in dialogue together. It is true that they could sustain almost any conversation, but there was no doubt that an essential dialogue was unfolding between them, which they maintained aloud before us all without giving cause for any objection. The lines of the drama that they substituted for ordinary language seemed made to order for that intimate colloquy. Truly, it was impossible to know where the constant stream of double meanings came from, since the author of the play had no reason to have foreseen such a situation. I became very uncomfortable. If I had not held in my hands a copy of *The Return of the Crusader* printed in Madrid in 1895, I would have believed that the play was written exclusively to bring about our ruin. As I have a good memory, I soon learned the five acts of the play. At night, in bed, I would torment myself before going to sleep with the most tender scenes.

The success of *The Return of the Crusader* was so great that all the spectators agreed they had never seen the like. A night of unforgettable art! Teresa and Gilbert were consecrated like two real artists. The public, moved even to the point of tears, experienced through their acting the highest emotions of a noble love filled with sacrifice.

As for me, I felt more at ease when I considered that the situation was somewhat out in the open now and no longer weighed only upon me. I felt myself supported by the public; as if Teresa's and Gilbert's love would be absolved and redeemed, and I could do nothing but adhere to that opinion. All of us were really forced to yield before that true love, which leaped over all social prejudices, free and sacred in its grandeur. One detail, which everyone remembers, sustained my illusion.

When the play was over and a really stunning ovation had kept the curtain up for several minutes, the actors decided to bring everybody out on stage. The director, the organizers, the orchestra conductor, and the man who painted the scenes received their just homage. Finally they made me climb up out of the pit. The public seemed enthusiastic at this gesture and the applause was stronger than ever. A fanfare was played and it all ended amid the joy and happiness of actors and audience. I interpreted the excessive applause as a final sanction: society had taken charge of everything and was disposed to share the drama's consequences with me to the end. Not long afterwards I was to realize the enormity of my error and the malevolent, uncomprehending attitude of that smug society.

As there was no reason to suspend Gilbert's visits to our house, they continued as before. Later they became daily. Before long we sensed a tide of calumny, envy, and insidious gossip against us. We have been attacked with the vilest weapons. Self-righteousness prevails among our critics: now one, now another devotes himself to stoning Teresa with his gossip. By the way, the other day a real stone fell on us. Can it be possible?

We were in the living room with the window open as usual. Gilbert and I were absorbed in one of our most intricate chess games, while Teresa was working near us on some crocheting. Suddenly, just as I was beginning to make a move, and apparently from very close by, a stone the size of a fist was thrown and fell noisily on the table, knocking over all the chess pieces. It was just as if a meteor had fallen on us. Teresa almost fainted and Gilbert turned very pale. I was the least disturbed at this inexplicable attempt. To calm them down, I said it must have been the prank of an irresponsible child. Nonetheless, we could no longer feel at ease and Gilbert left us soon afterwards. Personally, I didn't regret the incident too much with regard to our game, since a series of checks were leading my king into an inexorable checkmate.

With regard to my family situation, I must say that it has undergone an extraordinary change since *The Return of the Crusader*. Frankly, ever since the play was performed, Teresa has stopped being my wife and has become that strange and marvelous being who inhabits my house but is as far away as the stars. At the time of the play I began to have an inkling that she had been changing for some time, but so slowly that I had been unable to notice it.

My love for Teresa, that is, Teresa as my beloved, left a great deal to be desired. I confess without envy that Teresa's exaltation and the final awakening of her soul was a phenomenon beyond my control. With my love Teresa was resplendent. I saw her shine like a great crystal lamp. But it was a human and tolerable shine. Now Teresa dazzles me. I shut my eyes when she approaches and I only admire her from afar. I have the impression that since the night *The Return of the Crusader* was presented Teresa has not descended from the stage, and I think that perhaps she will never return to reality, to the simple, little, sweet reality we had before. She has completely forgotten it.

If it is true that each lover adorns and decorates the soul of his beloved, I must confess I am an artist with mediocre endowments for love. Like a clumsy sculptor, I saw Teresa's beauty, but only Gilbert has been able to bring it entirely out of its block. I recognize now that one is born for love as for any other art. We all aspire to achieve it, but it is conceded to very few. That is why love becomes a spectacle when it reaches perfection.

My love, like almost everyone else's, never went beyond the walls of our home. My courtship caught nobody's attention. On the contrary, Teresa and Gilbert are spied upon, followed step by step and minute by minute, as when they performed in the theatre and the quivering public waited in anguish for the outcome.

I remember what they say about Don Isidro, who painted the four evangelists on the curved triangles in the cupola of the parish church. Don Isidro never took the trouble to paint his pictures from the beginning. He put everything in the hands of an apprentice, and when the work was almost done, he picked up the brushes and with a few strokes transformed it into a work of art. Then he signed his name. The evangelists were his last work and they say that Don Isidro did not manage to give his masterly touch to St. Luke. Indeed, there is the saint, his beauty unrevealed, his expression puerile and somewhat uncertain. I cannot help thinking that if Gilbert had not come the same thing would have happened with Teresa. She would have remained mine forever, but without that final splendor that Gilbert has given her with his spirit.

Needless to say, our conjugal life has been completely interrupted. I dare not think about Teresa's body. It would be a profanation, a sacrilege. Formerly, our intimacy was complete and not subject to any system. I enjoyed her simply as one enjoys water and sun. Now that past seems incomprehensible and fabulous to me. I believe I am lying if I say that I used to hold Teresa in my arms, that incandescent Teresa, who now goes about the house with divine footsteps, doing domestic chores that do not succeed in making her seem human. Serving at the table, mending clothes, or sweeping, Teresa is a superior being who is completely unattainable. It would be totally erroneous to hope that just any dialogue would take us suddenly back to one of those sweet scenes of the past. And when I think that I could transform myself into a troglodyte and assault Teresa right now in the kitchen, I am paralyzed with horror.

On the other hand, I regard Gilbert almost as an equal, though he is the one who produced the miracle. My former feeling of inferiority has completely disappeared. I realize that in one act of my life I have risen to his heights. That act was choosing and loving Teresa. I chose her simply, as Gilbert himself would have done; indeed, I have the impression that I got there ahead of him, robbing him of the woman. For he would have had to love Teresa anyway, the first moment he found her. Our most profound affinity has been confirmed in her, and in that affinity I have taken precedence. However, I must also consider and accept the contrary idea that Teresa only loved me because she was dreaming of Gilbert and looking for him in me.

After we stopped seeing each other at the end of grammar school I always suffered in the thought that my achievements were on a much lower level than Gilbert's. Every time he came to town during vacations I carefully avoided him, refusing to compare my life with his.

But deeper down, if I seek the ultimate sincerity, I cannot complain of my destiny. I would not change the kind of humanity that I have known for the clientele of a doctor or a lawyer. The string of customers the length of the counter has been an inexhaustible field of experience for me, and I have consecrated my life to it with gusto. I have always been interested in people's behavior when they are buying, choosing, craving, and denying themselves. To make renouncing costly items bearable and acquiring something cheap pleasant has been one of my favorite endeavors. Besides, with a good part of my clientele I cultivate special relations that are a far cry from those ordinarily existing between merchants and buyers. The spiritual interchange between these persons and me is almost *de rigueur*. I am really pleased when somebody comes to my store to look for some article and goes home with heart refreshed by a confidential talk or fortified by a sane bit of advice.

I confess this without the least shadow of pride, since after all I am the one now supplying the theme for everyone's conversation. Trustingly, I have taken my private life and put it on the counter, as when I take a piece of cloth and stretch it out for my customer's close scrutiny.

There have even been some good people, excessive in their desire to help me, who devote themselves to spying on what happens at my house. As I have been unable to renounce their services voluntarily, I have learned that Gilbert makes visits in my absence. This has seemed incomprehensible to me. It is true that the other day Teresa told me that Gilbert had come to the house in the morning to pick up his cigarette case, which he had forgotten the night before. But now, according to my informers, Gilbert goes there about noon. Yesterday, no less, someone came to tell me I should go home that instant, if I wished to find out about everything. I roundly refused. Go home at twelve? I imagined how frightened Teresa would be seeing me come in at such an unaccustomed hour.

I declare that all my behavior is based on absolute trust. I must also say that common ordinary jealousies have not succeeded in taking hold of my spirit, not even in the most trying moments when Gilbert and Teresa have betrayed themselves by a glance, a gesture, or a silence. I have watched them become silent and confused, as if their souls had suddenly fallen to the ground, united, blushing and naked.

I don't know what they think or do or say when I'm not there. But I imagine them very easily silent, suffering, one far from the other, trembling, while I too start trembling here at the store, with them and for them.

Here we are waiting for some unfathomable event to put an end to this situation. For the moment, I am dedicated to putting obstacles in the way of the usual dénouements consecrated by custom, rejecting and suppressing all of them. Perhaps it is in vain to expect it, but I am trying to obtain a special dénouement for us, in keeping with our souls.

In any case, I must say that I have always felt a great repugnance for the idea of magnanimity. It's not that it displeases me as a virtue, since I admire it a great deal in others, but I cannot allow myself to exercise it, and above all against a person of my own family. The fear of being taken for a magnanimous man dispels any idea of sacrifice in my mind, making me decide to stick to my embarrassing role as obstacle and witness to the end. I know this role is now quite intolerable; nonetheless, I shall try to continue in it until violent circumstances eject me.

I know there are wives who get down on their knees and weep, their foreheads pressed against the ground, begging for forgiveness. If this should happen to me with Teresa, I'll abandon all and surrender. I shall finally be a deceived husband, and after my titanic battle too. God, give my spirit strength in the certainty that Teresa will not lower herself to such a scene!

In *The Return of the Crusader* all ends well because in the last act Griselda dies a poetic death, and the two rivals, brought together by their grief, lay down their violent swords and promise to end their lives in heroic battle. But here in real life everything is different.

All is perhaps over between us, yes, Teresa, but the curtain hasn't completely fallen and it is necessary to carry on at any price. I know that life has placed you in a grievous dilemma; perhaps you feel like an actress abandoned by the public on a stage without an exit. There are no more lines to recite and no prompter to help you; nevertheless, society is waiting and getting impatient and busy inventing tales that question your virtue. Here is a fine chance for you to improvise, Teresa.

He Did Good While He Lived

August 1st

I overturned a bottle of glue on my desk this afternoon a little before closing the office just after Pedro left. I had been very busy getting everything cleaned up and doing over four letters that were already signed. I also had to change the invoice on an account.

I could have left these tasks for tomorrow and entrusted them to Pedro; nevertheless, it seemed unfair to me. I thought he had enough to do with his own work.

Pedro is an excellent employee. He has served me for several years and I have no complaint against him. On the contrary, Pedro deserves, as an employee and as a person, my highest esteem.

Lately I have noticed that he is preoccupied, as if he wants to tell me something. I fear he is tired or discontented with his work. To lighten his labors a little, I propose from now on to lend him some help. As I had to do the stained letters over, I realized that I am not accustomed to the machine. Therefore, it will be useful for me to practice a little.

From tomorrow on, instead of an inconsiderate boss, Pedro will have a companion who helps him in his work, thanks to the fact that today I upset a bottle of glue and have made these reflections.

Knocking over the bottle was due to one of those inexplicable movements of my elbow that have cost me now so many headaches. (The other day I broke a flower vase at Virginia's.)

August 3rd

This diary must record disagreeable things too. Yesterday Mr. Gálvez came to my office and again proposed his shady deal. I am indignant. He dared to almost double his first offer, providing that I consent to put my profession at the service of his robbing.

An entire family stripped of its patrimony if I accept a handful of money! No, Mr. Gálvez. I am not the person you want. I absolutely refuse, and the usurer leaves asking me to keep this matter very secret.

And to think that Mr. Gálvez belongs to our Council! I have a little capital (it is nothing compared with Virginia's), built up penny by penny, and I shall never consent to increase it in an improper fashion.

For the rest, this has been a good day and during it I have shown that I am disposed to fulfill my proposals: to be a considerate boss to Pedro.

August 5th

I read with particular interest the books Virginia gives me. She has a library that is not very large but selected with taste. I have just read a book, *Reflections of a Christian Gentleman*, which doubtless belonged to Virginia's husband and which gives me a fine idea of her appreciation for good literature.

I aspire to be a worthy successor of this gentleman who, according to Virginia, always made a great effort to follow the wise teachings of the book.

August 6th

Virginia's friendship brings me great benefit by making me fulfill my social obligations.

Not without certain satisfaction I have just learned that the priest, during the session of the Council on Morality, which I did not attend because I was ill, praised my work in it as editor of *The Christian Voice*. This newspaper every month disperses the beneficent work of our group.

The Council on Morality occupies itself in propagating, illustrating, and exalting religion, as well as narrowly watching over our town's morals. It is also seriously concerned with the good of our culture, using all means within reach. From time to time there falls upon the Council the burden of smoothing away some of the economic obstacles that often confront our parish priest.

Because of the high quality of its aims, the Council is forced to demand, under threat of sanctions, exemplary conduct of its associates. When a member deviates in any way in his moral conduct from the rules in our statutes, he receives a first warning. If he does not mend his ways, he receives a second warning and then a third. This precedes his expulsion.

On the other hand, the Council has established worthy and esteemed distinctions for the members who fulfill their duties. It is satisfactory to recall that over the many years only a small number of warnings and one single expulsion have been necessary. And there are many persons whose honorable lives have been praised and described in the pages of *The Christian Voice*.

I like to refer to our Council in my diary. It occupies an important place in my life, next to my affection for Virginia.

August 7th

The fact that I write a diary is also due to Virginia. It is her idea. She has been writing her diary for many years and knows how to do it very well. She has such an original faculty for narrating facts that she embellishes them and makes them interesting. Of course, sometimes she exaggerates. For example, the other day she read me the description of a walk we took in the company of a family whose friendship we cultivate.

Now, this walk was just like any other; it even had its disagreeable aspects. The person carrying the food suffered a spectacular fall, and we found ourselves in the position of having to eat a deplorable mess of food. Virginia herself stumbled while were were walking over a rocky terrain, seriously hurting her foot. On our return an unexpected storm surprised us and we reached home all muddy and soaked through.

But the curious thing is that in Virginia's diary not only are these things not mentioned, but the facts in general seem to be singularly changed. The walk was enchanting from beginning to end. The mountains, the trees, and the sky are admirably described. There is even a murmuring little brook included that I don't remember having seen or heard. But the most important thing is that in the last part of the narration there is a dialogue that I did not have then and that I have never had with Virginia. There is no doubt that the dialogue is beautiful, but I don't recognize myself in it, and its contents seem to me—I don't know quite how to say it—a little inadequate for people of our age. Besides, I employ a poetic language that I am far from possessing.

Doubtless this reveals in Virginia a high spiritual capacity that is completely foreign to me. I can only say what happens to me or what I think, simply as it is. That is why my diary isn't the least bit interesting.

August 8th

Pedro is still a little reserved. He is being extremely diligent, and it seems to me there is something deliberate behind this. He wants to ask me for something and he is trying to satisfy me beforehand.

Thank goodness I have had some good business deals lately, and if Pedro is reasonable in his demands, I shall be glad to please him. A raise in salary? With great pleasure!

August 10th

The sixth anniversary of Virginia's husband's death. She has been kind enough to invite me to go with her to the cemetery.

The tomb is covered by an artistic and costly monument. It represents a seated woman weeping on a marble stone that she holds in her lap.

We found the meadow surrounding the tomb invaded by weeds. We busied ourselves in pulling them out and I managed to get a thorn in my finger.

As we were leaving, I discovered at the foot of the monument this beautiful inscription: *He Did Good While He Lived,* which I have decided to takè as a motto.

To do good, a fine objective now almost abandoned by men!

We returned late from the cemetery, walking in silence.

August 14th

I had a pleasant time at Virginia's. We chatted about different and amusing things. She played our favorite pieces on the piano.

All these visits produce a wholesome impression of happiness in me. I return from them with my spirit renewed and disposed toward good works. I give regularly to charity, but I would like to do a specific and perfectly directed good work. To help somebody in an efficient, constant way. As one helps someone one loves, a member of one's family, perhaps one's child—

August 16th

I remember with satisfaction that it has been a year today since I began to write these notes.

A year of my life placed before my eyes thanks to the fair soul who watches over and orients my actions. Undoubtedly, God has put her like a guardian angel on my path.

Virginia beautifies everything she touches. Now I understand why everything appears beautiful and different in her diary.

On the day of our walk, while I was foolishly sleeping under a tree, she was contemplating the marvels of the landscape and later dazzled me with her description of it. From now on I'm also going to try to open my eyes to beauty and record its images. Perhaps then I shall be able to write a diary as beautiful as Virginia's.

August 17th

Before shutting my eyes to the world's vulgarities and turning to the sole contemplation of beauty, I must make a slight clarification of an economic nature.

For a period that I consider immemorial (I didn't know Virginia then) I have always worn a certain brand of hat. These hats, of excellent foreign make, have been going up continually in price. A hat is not a thing that wears out in a short time, but I have bought a half dozen at least in the last years. Taking six hats as a base, and a progressive increase of five pesos in the price of each, I make the following calculations: if the last hat cost me forty pesos, the first must have cost only fifteen. Adding up the successive differences in each purchase, I realize that my loyalty to one brand has cost me seventy pesos up to now.

I have no objection to the quality of these new hats; they are splendid. But my lack of economy seems to me deplorable. If I initially chose a hat costing fifteen pesos, I should have always kept to that fixed price and not let myself be carried away by the increasing greediness of merchants and manufacturers. I must recognize that hats have always been available at that price.

Because I need to get a new hat, I am going to put things in their proper place: I shall suddenly jump from one price to another, saving twenty-five pesos.

August 18th

The only fifteen-peso hat I could find in my size is of a greenish color and rather poorly made.

Out of simple curiosity, I asked the price of my ex-favorite make. It is no less than fifty pesos. So much the better! As far as I'm concerned, it can cost two hundred, since from now on I have resolved to be modest in my hats.

I reflect that I have made a saving. In my business God's help continues manifest. On the other hand, the Council is experiencing difficult circumstances. It has taken on the task of paving our parish church with new tiles and it needs the support of its members more than ever.

I have decided to make a donation. Tomorrow I'm going to see the priest, who in addition to being spiritual director and founder of our Council, is its treasurer at the moment.

August 19th

The priest flatters me with an affable and protective friendship. He makes a great effort to get to know my problems and finds just the right solutions for all of them. He possesses great ingenuity and likes to speak of things with subtle allusions. According to him, I have done nothing so far in my life to regret. My friendship with Virginia receives his blessing and is inspired with his paternal advice.

As soon as he found out the object of my visit, his kindness knew no bounds, and he said that with such children the house of God would be maintained safe and beautiful in our city.

I think I have done a good work and my heart is satisfied.

August 20th

The little wound I got when we went to the cemetery has not healed over. It seems to be infected and has developed into a painful swelling. As I have heard that wounds received in the proximity of cadavers can be dangerous, I have gone to see the doctor.

I had to endure a simple but trying cure. Virginia has been concerned and shows me her affection with delicate attentions.

At the office Pedro continues being cautious, as if awaiting an opportunity.

August 22nd

A page devoted to our honorable Council: I have just been honored with a distinction granted very few of our members. My name now figures in the list of Meritorious Members and I have been given a beautiful diploma which contains my nomination.

The priest pronounced a beautiful speech during which he evoked the memory of some Meritorious Members now deceased, inviting us to follow their example. He lingered with particular interest praising Virginia's husband, whom he described as one of the most illustrious members the group has had.

Naturally, I am very content. Virginia herself has increased my satisfaction by showing how proud she is of the honor I have just received.

The only thing darkening this happy day is the following fact: one of the people who was most insistent about my election to the category of Meritorious Member was Mr. Gálvez, a person I no longer esteem and whose sincerity I doubt.

But after all, perhaps he regrets what he proposed to me and is trying to ingratiate himself with me. If that is the case, I shall make it up with him. I have kept absolutely quiet about his shady deals.

August 26th

Pedro has finally made up his mind. What he had to tell me is nothing less than this: he is leaving.

He is leaving the last day of the month and he has been putting off telling me all month long until now it's almost over. I have only a few days left to find a replacement for him.

I realize that Pedro is right. He is leaving our town in search of broader horizons. And he is right. A serious and hard-working boy has the right to look for advancement. I'm resigned to losing him and I'm giving him a letter of recommendation. (I intend to grant him a bonus.)

Now I have to look for a replacement worthy of Pedro, which won't be easy at all.

August 27th

For some time now I have intended to hire a secretary whenever Pedro might leave my services. I think I have a good candidate.

I am acquainted with a young woman who seems very suitable. An orphan, she makes her living by sewing for wealthy families. I know this work tires her out and that she is not fond of it. She is a very serious girl and comes from an honorable family. She lives with her old paralytic aunt.

This evening Virginia dismissed my candidate rather lightly. I don't wish to contradict her, but it seems to me that she has been rather unjust.

Nonetheless, I'll consult with the priest. He knows everyone and will tell me if it's a good idea to take her on as a secretary.

August 30th

One plans things but God decides them. This morning when I was getting ready to leave to look for the priest, I found myself stopped at the door of my office by none other than the young lady I had chosen for the job.

I just needed to look at her face again to decide to give her the job. It is a face that expresses suffering.

Maria appears at least five years older than she really is. Her face is sad to contemplate, faded before its time. Her reddened eyes are proof of nights passed in sewing. Why she might even lose her eyesight! (At this moment it pains me to recall Virginia's words.)

I tell the young lady to come back tomorrow, that perhaps I can give her a job. She is very grateful and before leaving says to me, "Oh, I hope you can help me!"

These are simple, frank, even commonplace words. Still, when I think about them, I decide that I can help her, that I *must* help her.

September 4th

My moral responsibility in the Council continues to grow. In the last issue of *The Christian Voice* I had to publish an article by Mr. Gálvez. He pays me clear praise in it, though indirectly. Apparently, Mr. Gálvez seems determined to regain my friendship.

In that same journal, which has a literary section, there appears under the pseudonym Fidelia a little poem composed by Virginia. I had asked her for it a few days before, without telling her my intentions. I think I have given her a pleasant surprise. The composition brought eulogies from the priest.

September 7th

A small but significant disaster has happened to me. I'll just have to accept it.

Wishing to distract myself a little and to aid my digestion, I took a short walk when I finished my meal. I went further than necessary, and finding myself on the outskirts of town, I was surprised by rain. As it wasn't a hard rain, I returned slowly without worrying about it. When I was only two blocks from home, it started coming down so heavily that I got drenched from head to toe.

And my brand-new hat! When I went to look for it after putting it out to dry, I found it converted into a shapeless, rebellious mass that refused to go on my head.

I had to replace it with my old hat, that has endured sun and rain for more than three years.

September 10th

Maria has turned out to be an excellent secretary. Pedro was always a good employee, but without any offense to him I can affirm that Maria is better. She has a special happy way of doing her work, and it gives me pleasure to see her always active and contented. Only on her face the traces of the old weariness remain.

September 14th

The abominable Mr. Gálvez has returned to my office. After a hearty embrace, he calls me two or three times by my name of Meritorious.

Mr. Gálvez is an excellent conversationalist; he spends a great deal of time jumping from one topic to another. I listen to him spellbound, and when I least expect it, he brings up his "deal."

After innumerable beatings about the bush and circumlocutions, Mr. Gálvez excuses himself very frankly for having dared to settle the remuneration for me in the deal that he is proposing. He asks me to decide how much I want, taking into account the kind of matter it is.

My only answer is to invite Mr. Gálvez to leave the office.

This time I didn't promise to keep quiet at all and I couldn't help telling Virginia the whole story.

September 17th

A bachelor's life is always filled with difficulties and inconveniences. Especially if the bachelor has as his guide a book like *Reflections of the Christian Gentleman*. I almost venture to say that for a celibate man it is impossible to lead a virtuous life.

Nevertheless, one can try. As my marriage to Virginia is not far off (about six months away), I am trying to keep to certain disciplines, so as to arrive at the marriage in a relative state of purity.

I still have hopes that I can become the type of Christian gentleman that Virginia's husband ought to be. That is what I am striving for now.

September 21st

I have always felt a great emptiness in my heart. It is true that Virginia fills my existence, but there still remains that empty feeling.

Virginia is not a person I can protect. Rather, I should say, she protects me, poor lonely fellow that I am. (My mother died fifteen years ago.)

Now, that protective instinct is still there and calls out from the very depths of my being. I harbor the illusion of having a child, a child who would receive that unused tenderness, who would respond to my obscure and paternal call.

Sometimes I thought about turning that affectionate current toward Pedro. But he never gave me even the filial opportunity of reproaching him. He always widened the barrier I was trying to cross with his diligent employee's conduct—

September 25th

Virginia is the president of "Toys for the Poor," a feminine association dedicated to collecting funds during the year for the distribution of toys among needy children at Christmastime. Now she is very busy organizing a series of festivals with the object of surpassing the record of previous years.

Without realizing the importance of my occupations and undoubtedly guided by her good sentiments, Virginia asked me to take the direction of these festivities under my charge. Very regretfully, I made her see that my present duties, profession, the Council, and the *Voice* did not permit me to oblige her.

She did not seem to heed my excuses, and half-seriously, half-jokingly, she complained about my lack of humanity.

September 27th

I am really confused. Discretion is my forte and I like to demand it of the people I admire.

Today I received a letter from Mr. Gálvez, a dry and offensive, yet cleverly attentive letter. In it he simply invites me to keep silent about what he calls "a serious matter between honorable people." He is referring to that nasty proposal of his. I don't know up to what point the word "honorable" can possibly be stretched; however elastic it may be, it can not include both Mr. Gálvez and me.

His letter ends in this fashion: "I shall be grateful to you for recommending discretion to a certain person with regard to this matter." And he dares to sign: "Your affectionate and attentive friend and co-member, etc."

Ah, Virginia, how I come to know your defects to my sorrow. Mr. Gálvez is doubtless right. He is a rascal, but he is right. He also is within his rights to demand my reserve. I'll do what I can. I shall see to it that his behavior is not divulged.

September 28th

Before, that is to say, until very recently, I didn't dare to conceive of Virginia with defects. Proceeding now in a logical and human fashion, I shall try to find out, study, and pardon her defects, hoping that one day she can remedy them. For the time being I shall just expose this trait: Virginia has a habit of guiding herself by "what people say" and she always goes by the general opinion.

For example, when she speaks of someone she never says: "This or the other seems to me," but invariably expresses: "They say about so-and-so, they told me this or that about so-and-so, I heard this said about so-and-so." That is the way it goes constantly.

The other day Virginia said, referring to Maria's sewing: "Perhaps I'm mistaken, but with all that going in and out of people's houses she did, certain things were said about her."

October 1st

The priest, who extends his vigilance over the Council on Morality, despite the fact that he is its guide and spiritual chief, wants it to have an independent management.

Today we had an important meeting. A new interim president had to be elected due to the prolonged absence of the person who occupied the chair of vice-president. (Our president died at the beginning of this year, may he rest in peace.)

Contrary to what normally happens in our Council, the task of electing a president became embarrassing by virtue of a lamentable coincidence, which has been repeated the last four years with frightful regularity.

Our last four presidents have died at the beginning of the year, shortly after their nomination. Among the members a superstitious fear of occupying the presidency has been developing.

Now, being a question of an interim president, the problem didn't seem so grave. Nonetheless, even the persons who by their scant intellectual capacity were free from any danger of nomination clearly manifested their nervousness.

After their election, two members renounced the honorable charge, alleging their lack of merit or time to undertake it.

The Council was in jeopardy, and an insistent and anxious fear pervaded the large gathering. The priest seemed extremely nervous and from time to time mopped his brow with his handkerchief.

The results of the third vote, awaited almost like a sentence, designated as interim president none other than Mr. Gálvez. A burst of applause, this time greater than before, accompanied the announcement given with a tremulous voice by the priest. To everyone's astonishment, Mr. Gálvez not only accepted his election, but thanked us effusively as though it were an "unmerited distinction." He offered to work diligently for the good of our cause, and toward this end he solicited the support of all the members, but especially the cooperation of the Meritorious Members.

The priest heaved a sigh of relief and mopped his brow with the handkerchief a last time, answering Mr. Gálvez by saying that we had before our eyes a "heroic legionary of the Christian hosts."

The session was adjourned in the midst of general satisfaction. I recall with repugnance the embrace of congratulation that I was forced to give Mr. Gálvez.

October 5th

I have realized that I can never be like Virginia and that I shouldn't like to be either.

To see only beauty one must shut one's eyes completely to reality. Life offers a beautiful background landscape, but unfolds thousands of sad or dirty facts over it.

October 7th

I think this business of writing diaries is in fashion. I discovered accidentally on Maria's desk a little book which, by chance, was open before my eyes. I realized they were personal notes and I wanted to shut the book. But I couldn't help reading some words that became engraved on my mind, and here they are: "My boss is very good to me. For the first time in my life I feel the protection of a kind person."

The realization that I was doing something very wrong was stronger than my unpardonable curiosity. I left the book lying where it was and was plunged in a state of perplexity.

So there is somebody in the world whom I protect? I felt myself close to tears. I evoked Maria's sweet face with the deep circles under her eyes, and I felt surge from my heart a long restrained emotion.

Really, I must pay a little more attention to her, do something which will justify the confidence she has in me. For the moment, I am going to exchange the ugly table she has for a modern desk.

October 10th

My visits to Virginia's house take place in such a normal fashion that I am not going to describe them.

I am slightly annoyed with her. Lately she has acquired the habit of making certain recommendations to me. Now, for example, she referred to a distracted air I adopt when I walk and that, according to her, makes me stumble into people and often even into posts. Besides, Virginia has simultaneously acquired a parrot and a little dog.

The parrot doesn't know how to talk yet and utters disagreeable shrieks. Virginia's greatest delight consists in teaching it to say some words, my name among them, a thing I don't like.

These are just trifles, I know, things without importance that do not damage her image nor diminish my affection. Nonetheless, when I am able to, I shall try to correct them.

October 11th

The dog is just as annoying as the parrot. Last night, while Virginia was playing the *Dance of the Hours* on the piano, the little beast patiently applied himself to destroying my hat. When the destruction was ended he came running into the living room with the band and the lining in his mouth. It is true that my hat was old, but I didn't like Virginia laughing at the situation.

This time I didn't try to make calculations, and in view of the poor results of my past economy, I bought a hat of my favorite make. I shall be careful with it when I go to Virginia's.

October 15th

The priest, taking advantage of the fact that we accidentally met each other on the street, told me he thinks Virginia and I should put forward the date of our marriage. This time he did not employ his system of delicate allusions to which he is so addicted.

In conclusion he told me that Virginia's properties need more careful attention.

I don't see any just reason for advancing the date; nevertheless, I shall talk with her about it. Regarding the property, I wish to pay great attention to it, but on a strictly professional basis.

October 18th

I have just learned an astonishing thing: Virginia's husband left three illegitimate children at his death.

I would have refused to believe such a thing if it hadn't been a responsible person who told me. The mother of those children has also died, and they live, therefore, in the most complete abandonment. They wander about barefoot through the market and manage to live some way or other, performing humiliating chores.

An anguishing question assails me: can Virginia know about it? And if she knows, can she keep on distributing toys with a clear conscience while her husband's children are dying of starvation?

Virginia's husband! A Meritorious Member of the Council! The assiduous reader of the *Reflections!* I decide to find out some things.

October 19th

I cannot believe in Virginia's husband's salvation after having contemplated the three emaciated, roguish versions of his face. The dead man's serious expression appears in these faces very deformed by hunger and misery, but it is still quite recognizable.

I haven't been able to do anything yet for these children, but as soon as I get married, I will be responsible for their well-being. Somehow or other I intend to speak to Virginia about this situation which dishonors the name she still bears.

October 24th

Each day Maria writes down something to increase my esteem for her. She has made important improvements in the office and has an instinct for order. Our old method for filing correspondence has been changed to a modern and better system. The old typewriter has disappeared, and in its place there is a new one that is a delight to use. The furniture is placed in more convenient spots and the whole office looks more agreeable and rejuvenated.

Maria is contented at her new desk, but the suffering look remains on her face. I ask her: "Something wrong, miss? Are you still working at night?" She smiles weakly and responds: "No, nothing's wrong, nothing—"

October 25th

I have reflected that Maria's salary is by no means what it should be. I suspect that she is still sewing and staying up nights.

As I had taken her under my indirect protection, I resolved to increase her salary this morning. She seemed so upset when she thanked me that I fear I have hurt her. Looking for a secretary, I have come upon a beautiful feminine soul.

Besides, Maria's pale face is the purest semblance of womankind I have ever contemplated.

October 27th

My bachelor life is coming to its end. Not four months, but just two, are left before I marry Virginia. Last night we agreed on it, following the priest's suggestion.

I tried to take advantage of the opportunity to speak to her about the children, but there was no way to do it. She went on again eulogizing her husband.

She must surely be ignorant of the children's existence. How can I speak to her of such a matter?

October 28th

The idea that I'm going to get married doesn't seem nearly as pleasing as it did from a distance. The bachelor in me doesn't die easily.

Not that I'm discontented with Virginia. Looking at it calmly, I think she responds to the ideal I have formed. Of course, she has her defects. There is her lack of discretion and the capriciousness of her judgment. But this is not serious. So I'm marrying a virtuous woman and I ought to be satisfied.

October 30th

Today I learned two things that tend to prematurely embitter my matrimonial life. They come from a feminine source, and because of that, they are not to be trusted. But their content is disturbing. The first is this: Virginia knows all about the abandoned children, their origin and their misery.

The second item is of an intimate nature and refers to Virginia's misfortune as a mother. I learned from her that her two children died when small. Well now, I have just learned that neither child reached the point of being born. At least not in the normal way.

With regard to these two pieces of news, I must say I am incredulous, and I see in them only the treachery of evil talk. That evil talk which corrodes and destroys small towns, disintegrating their elements. That anonymous and general zeal for damaging reputations by circulating the false coin of slander.

(In this house my cook Prudence is like a barometer that registers all the moral temperatures in the neighborhood.)

October 31st

All my mental capacities are grappling with the grave economic and material problems evoked by my approaching marriage. How time goes by!

Impossible here to give an inventory of all my worries. This diary no longer makes sense. As soon as I get married, I must destroy it. (No, perhaps I'll keep it as a memory of my bachelor days.)

November 9th

Something serious is happening around me. Yesterday I scarcely suspected anything. Today my tranquility is gone.

I would swear that there is something in the air, that some unknown event has suddenly plunged me into the center of general speculation. I feel that while walking down the street I awaken a trickle of curiosity, that then unfolds into a torrent of malevolent comments behind my back. And it's not to do with my marriage, everybody knows about that, and nobody is interested in it. No, this is something else and I think that the storm was unleashed today during High Mass, which I usually attend. Yesterday I still enjoyed peace, and now—

I came from church almost in flight, pursued by the curious glances, and I have been here for hours wondering what the cause of all this can be. I haven't had the nerve to go out on the street.

Well, isn't my conscience clean? Have I robbed? Killed? I must sleep peacefully. My life is as clean as a bright mirror.

November 10th

What a day, good Lord, what a day! What crime have I committed to live through it?

I got up early after hardly getting any sleep and went to the office a little after my usual hour. Along the way malicious glances again followed me. I thought I would lose my mind. But in the office I calmed down a bit. I was safe and I worked out a plan of investigation.

Suddenly the door opened and Maria, whom I scarcely recognized, came in. She was out of breath, like someone fleeing from great danger who takes refuge in the first doorway. Her face was paler than ever and the deep shadows under her eyes were like two spots of death in her pallor.

I helped her to sit down. I was upset. She looked me intensely in the eye and burst into tears.

She wept silently like one giving in to an emotion that has been restrained a long time and can no longer be repressed. Her weeping moved me so that I couldn't even speak. Her body was convulsed by sobs, her head shuddered between her moist hands, and she cried as if she were expiating the evils of the world.

I forgot everything contemplating her. My eye ran over her agitated body and stopped in astonishment at the curve of her belly.

My thoughts went from shadow to light in a grievous fashion.

Her belly, slightly swollen, little by little gave me all the clues to the drama.

In my throat an exclamation fluttered and came out in a sob. Unfortunate girl!

Maria was no longer weeping. Her face was beautiful with an inhuman, pitiful beauty. She kept silent, knowing there were no words on earth to convince a man of her innocence.

She also knew that destiny, love and misery were not enough to excuse a woman who had lost her purity.

She knew too that there were no human words to surpass the language that silence and weeping expressed. She knew this and kept silent. She placed it all in my hands, her only hope in me.

Outside the world stumbled, was shattered, banished. The true universe was in this room and had slowly sprung from my heart.

I don't know how long our colloquy lasted nor how it was interrupted by ordinary language. All I know is that Maria counted on me to the end.

Shortly afterwards I received two letters, posthumous messages from the world I inhabited. The poles of that world, Virginia and the Council, joined in a general clamor, charging me with dishonorable conduct.

Those two letters produced neither indignation nor sorrow in me; they belonged to a past in which nothing matters to me any more.

I realize that it is unnecessary to be cultured and learned to understand why justice does not exist in the world and why we all give up trying to exercise it. In order to be just, one must sacrifice one's own well-being many times.

As I am unable to reform the laws of the world or remake the human heart, I must submit and become adjusted. I must abandon my hard-won truths and return to the world and its lies.

So I go to see the priest. This time I shall not go seeking advice, but to make the air that I need breatheable, to pursue my right to continue being a man, though it be at the price of falsehood.

November 11th

After my interview with the priest, the Council will no longer be obliged to send me its warnings. I have made the confession of sin that they demanded.

If I had consented to abandon a wretched girl to her own disgrace, I would now enjoy the restoration of my reputation and my advantageous marriage. But I haven't even thought about Maria's guilt in her misfortune. It is enough for me to know that some-body took shelter under my wing at the most critical time of her life.

I am happy because I have discovered that I was living under a false and trivial interpretation of existence. I realize that the ideal of chivalry I was forcing myself to attain does not coincide with man's real sentiments.

If Virginia, instead of sending her nasty letter, had said, "I don't believe it," I would never have discovered that I was living a false life.

November 26th

Maria used to go to sew in all the best homes of the city. Per-haps in one of them lives the sneaky rascal who by his villainy brought to the surface the man I, unwittingly, was capable of being.

That rascal cannot take the child Maria carries in her womb away from me, for I have made it mine before human and divine laws.

Poor laws, continually flouted, that have lost their primitive and lofty significance.

November 29th

This morning Mr. Gálvez, the interim president of the Council on Morality, died.

His sudden death has caused a profound impression, because he was a long way from being old and he took a certain gusto in doing good works. (The beautiful chancel of the parish is due to him.) His reputation, however, was never very clean because of his loan-shark deals.

I myself sometimes judged his conduct severely, and though I had experiences to support these judgments, I believe I was a little harsh on him. Solemn funeral rites are being prepared for him. May God pardon him.

November 30th

This afternoon when we saw Mr. Gálvez's funeral cortège pass by our window, I noticed Maria's face change. It took on a grieved look, then the flickering of a faint smile. Then tears sprang to her eyes and she gently leaned her head against my chest.

Oh Lord, oh Lord, I will pardon all, I will forget all, but let me feel this joy!

December 22nd

After the death of its fifth president, the Council on Morality found itself in grave danger of succumbing. The priest had to come to the realization that only a suicidal person would take on the presidency.

Thanks to a clever measure, the Council has survived. It functions now by means of a directors' board made up of eight responsible people.

I have been invited to form part of this board, but I felt obliged to decline the offer. I have a young woman by my side I must take care of and tend. I am not in the mood for more councils and directors' boards—

December 24th

I think about the three miserable tots wandering about the city, while I am getting ready to receive a child who was also destined to be abandoned.

Begotten without love, they will be buffeted here and there like leaves by the winds of chance, while there in the cemetery on a beautiful monument an inscription is getting dark under the moss.